WILD
MILK

Earlier versions of some of these stories first appeared in:
American Short Fiction, The Believer, The Bennington Review, Black Warrior Review, B O D Y, Catapult, The Collagist, Gulf Coast, jubilat, Lana Turner: A Journal of Poetry & Opinion, Tin House, Poets.org, and in the anthologies *My Mother She Killed Me, My Father He Ate Me: Forty New Fairy Tales* (Penguin), *The New Census: An Anthology of Contemporary American Poetry* (Rescue Press), and *Poets on Teaching: A Sourcebook* (University of Iowa Press).

The publisher wishes to thank Robin Tripp.

ISBN: 978-0-9973666-8-6

Art on cover © Li Shan Chong, 2018
"Portrait of Lily Jane Fools"
Used by kind permission of the artist

Design and composition by Danielle Dutton
Printed on permanent, durable, acid-free recycled paper
in the United States of America

Dorothy, a publishing project books are distributed to the trade
by New York Review Books

Dorothy, a publishing project | St. Louis, MO
DOROTHYPROJECT.COM

WILD
MILK

SABRINA ORAH MARK

DOROTHY, A PUBLISHING PROJECT

for Noah Juniper and Eli Winter
my moon and my sun

"Dear incomprehension, it's thanks to you
I'll be myself in the end."
Samuel Beckett, *The Unnamable*

STORIES

WILD MILK

On the first day of Live Oak Daycare, all the children are given shovels and a small bag of dirt. "We encourage the children—even the babies, *especially* the babies—to work hard, imaginatively." Miss Birdy, my son's teacher, winks. She sits my baby boy in the middle of the floor with his shovel and dirt. He is not even a year old. I look around. The babies are happy. I have never seen such happy babies. Chewing on their shovels. Spreading around their dirt. Miss Birdy gives me a hug. I wave goodbye to my boy, but he doesn't see me. "Go, go," says Miss Birdy. "He's in good hands." She shows me her hands. They remind me, for some reason, of my hands.

Three hours later, I come to pick up my boy. He is wearing a bright orange poncho that does not belong to him. He crawls toward me, like a searchlight.

"Your child," says Miss Birdy, "is a phenomenon." I blush. "Oh, thank you. We too think he is very special," I say. I want to ask about the poncho, but Miss Birdy goes on. "I mean, your child is a mana mana," says Miss Birdy. "What I mean to say is that your child is a real man." Miss Birdy softly pinches her tongue and pulls off a long white hair. "Oh, that's better," she says. "I mean, a ma." She makes little, tiny spits. "I mean, a no one. Your child," says Miss Birdy, "is a real no one. No, no. That's not it either." Miss Birdy smoothes her stiff cotton skirt. It's pink with tiny red cherries on it. "What I mean to say, most of all," says Miss Birdy, "is that I love not being dead." "Me too," I say. "Oh, good!" says Miss Birdy. "Here's his bottle. He drank all his milk and then cried and cried and cried for more."

In the hallway, I pass a mother covered in daughters. I count five. I hold up my bundled son, like a form of identification. Like he will provide me safe passage across the border. "No daughters?" she asks. "No," I say. "No daughters." "How come?" she asks. She seems to be blaming me, unfairly. "By the time they arrived," I explain, "the daughters had turned." "Rotten?" she asks. "Not exactly rotten but gigantic." I hand her my boy so I can spread my arms wide. To show her how big. I take my boy back. "Gigantic," I repeat. "And mealy. I sent the whole bin back. The whole bin of daughters back. The brave thing would've been to keep them, I know, but they seemed so impossible to name." The mother nods. She still seems to disapprove, but before I can be certain her daughters lift her up, hungrily, and carry her away.

The strange thing about being a mother is how often I'm interrupted. Like something is happening and then something else is happening. It is difficult to get a good grasp on things.

The next day Miss Birdy is peeling vegetables. The babies are watching, transfixed. I have come early to pick up my boy, but I don't see my boy. Miss Birdy points to a child the color of chicken broth. "Yours?" she asks. "Definitely not mine," I say. She points to another and another, as if I lost my ticket for the coat check. I don't see my boy. It is becoming difficult to breathe and I am suddenly freezing cold. The floor opens up beneath me and just as I begin to fall through my boy crawls out from underneath a bassinet. In his fist is a tiny book. On the cover is a picture of a plain brown mouse. He holds it up. "MOUSE," he says. This is his first real word. "MY MOUSE," he says. I am amazed. I am relieved. His pronunciation is perfect. I want to pick him up. Reward him with kisses. Hold him and never let him go. But Miss Birdy stops me. "No, no," she says. She softly wags a finger at my boy. "That's not your mouse. That's no one's mouse." Her voice slows. "That mouse—" Miss Birdy coughs. "That mouse," she says, "is alone in this world, and barely . . ." Miss Birdy stops. "What was that?" she asks. "What was what?" I say. "That sound," says Miss Birdy. "I don't know," I say. "What did it sound like?" "It was a sound that sounded like a sound," says Miss Birdy. "Like a sound a sound would make. Never mind. Where was I?" "You were with the mouse." "Oh, the mouse! Do you know him?" "No," I say. "Unless you mean . . ." "Neither do I," says Miss Birdy. "And this is my point. That mouse . . ." Miss Birdy is now looking at my boy. "That mouse is alone in this world and barely . . ." Miss Birdy sucks in one long, beautiful breath. "Exists," says Miss Birdy, triumphantly. "That mouse is not unlike you." She is still looking at my boy. "When I call out for that mouse in the dark does the mouse come? No, the mouse does not. Do you? So far not even once." My baby puts his whole hand in Miss Birdy's mouth and leaves it there for what seems like days.

On Monday Miss Birdy's bright pink blouse is fluttering with excitement. "Your boy wrote his name today all by himself!" She hands me a piece of construction paper. Someone, not my baby, has written on it S H R E D S. I hand the paper back. "That is not his name." "Oh," says Miss Birdy. She looks at the paper and her face crumples. "I am sorry," says Miss Birdy. "I don't know how this happened." "I don't know how anything happens," I say. We hold hands. "I'm so lonely," says Miss Birdy. "I'm so lonely too," I say. "I thought you were my hiding place," says Miss Birdy. I picture her skull. "I thought you were mine," I say. Miss Birdy ties a yellow scarf around her head. "Stop picturing my skull," says Miss Birdy. She is clearly upset. Her lips are cracked and begin to bleed a little. She looks at the construction paper and traces each letter with her thumb. "If this isn't his name, then whose name is it?" She sorts through the other babies. She pats me down as if searching for something. She touches me on the thigh. She feels like she's about to snow.

The next day, there's a message from Miss Birdy. "We cannot give your boy his bottle. The milk you left was wild. Please bring better milk."

I rush to Live Oak. I have no better milk. This is the only milk I have. I point to each breast. Miss Birdy is holding my baby. He is shivering and hungry. Miss Birdy is snowing. Hard. I try to walk toward her but there is a great wind and I can barely see through the big, white flakes. "THIS IS THE ONLY MILK I HAVE." I am calling to Miss Birdy and my boy through the snowstorm. My arms are outstretched. "Come to Mama," I cry. I say my baby's name. It sounds smaller and flatter than I ever imagined it. I can't get to him. Miss Birdy is a blizzard that could last all winter. "I AM SORRY." I am shouting. Miss Birdy has my baby and she is snowing. It is all my fault. I should never have left him. I AM SORRY I AM SORRY I AM SORRY. I am punching at the snow. I am fighting against nature when I know I have no choice but to wait until spring. The mother covered in daughters kneels beside me. This time I count fifteen. "Climb on," she says. "I am so sorry," I say. "It is the only milk I have." "Of course it is," she says. "Is there room?" I ask. "Around my neck," she says. I climb up and hang on loosely. The mother covered in daughters is warm and I am so tired. "Go to sleep," says the mother. "I will wake you up when it's time to go." But the mother never does wake me up. Which is how you know this story is true.

TWEET

A lot of my friends are following the Rabbi so I start following the Rabbi too. We follow him into a community swimming pool and splash around. Our suits match. Light blue with moons and stars. The Rabbi's twinkle so ours twinkle too. When the Rabbi floats we all float too. A lot of my friends are following the Rabbi out of the swimming pool, so I follow the Rabbi too. We wrap ourselves in one large, green towel. The towel is tagged. We take turns touching the tag. God, it is lovely. It is a lovely, lovely tag. That we should all one day be tagged by a tag as lovely as this tag. That we should one day run into one another on this or that sidewalk and know we once were friends. Good friends.

At the community swimming pool there is a goat. There should not be a goat but one thing has led us to another. So now there is a goat. The Rabbi climbs inside. We follow him. It is warm. Too warm. Beautiful Leonora is here. She is following the Rabbi too. We nod to each other. Inside the goat is a tree. The goat is tagged. The tree is tagged. The Rabbi sits under its shade. The shade is tagged. We sit next to the Rabbi. We breathe in the matted, gamey heat. We are sweating. We pick at the stars on our suits. We leave the moons alone. We pick at the Rabbi's stars. We leave the moons alone. He doesn't seem to notice or care or feel us picking at his suit. We are struggling to be recognized. We wish for a short lecture on god and happiness. We wish Beautiful Leonora would get out of here, for she is in our way. For she is tons more beautiful than the beauty of all of our faces combined. Someone bursts out laughing and disappears. Still, without Beautiful Leonora it is crowded enough.

The Rabbi reaches up as if to wave at us, almost smiles, but then his hand drops and our hearts sink. The heat inside this goat is unbearable. The Rabbi climbs out so we climb out too.

On Wednesday my friends follow the Rabbi all the way to 125th Street so I follow too. It's a clear, sunny afternoon. Today my friends and I are a merry gang. The Rabbi walks slowly so we all walk slowly. When the Rabbi stops we all stop too. At around four o'clock we get so close to the Rabbi we almost catch a nectarine that falls out of his wool pocket, but Beautiful Leonora gets to it first. We wish Beautiful Leonora would get the hell out of our way. We wish this Rabbi bore gusto, but he bears none.

The Rabbi sighs. The Rabbi is morose. "A Mouse Rabbi?" we ask. "No," we say. "A morose Rabbi." We get a faraway look. "A Mouse Rabbi?" we ask. "Once," we say. "Long ago."

Nobody asks this Rabbi for comfort, only that he should guide us.

We follow the Rabbi. His sighs get louder. We follow him into a brick building and up a carpeted stairway that eventually leads to Apartment B. The Rabbi knocks. We are piled up all over the hallway. We are sleeping. We are reading. We are becoming very famous, or getting married, or slowly dying. The Rabbi knocks again. Beautiful Leonora answers. How has she gotten here first? Who is following whom? We look behind us. Endless grass. A person could get lost in this grass.

A lot of my friends are following A Person Could Get Lost In This Grass so I start following A Person Could Get Lost In This Grass too.

There is so much grass here. In the distance, we see My Mother. We try to run toward her but the grass slows us down. For days, we follow A Person Could Get Lost In This Grass until we finally come to My Mother. She is bent over, like she is picking a flower. We tap her on the shoulder. When she turns around we see she is not My Mother, but Beautiful Leonora. Her mouth is stuffed with grass, and she is smiling, and she is more beautiful than ever.

A lot of my friends are following Apartment B so I start following Apartment B where Beautiful Leonora and the morose Rabbi are now slow dancing. "What song is that?"

we ask. We listen. We stare at Beautiful Leonora. She is grass-stained and far better than us. "It Had To Be You," we say. "Who?" we say. "Me?" "No," we say. "The name of the song," we say. "It Had to Be You." "You?" we ask. "Us?" we hope. "No," we say. "Her." We point at Beautiful Leonora. It had to be her, which doesn't seem fair. It really should be all of us.

Though we refuse to follow Beautiful Leonora, we drag ourselves over to her, she who is light incarnate, and say, "Beautiful Leonora, it really should be all of us." We try to push her away. We try to slow dance with the Rabbi. A lot of my friends are following It Had to Be You so I start following It Had to Be You too. We are pushing and shoving and trying to get ourselves close to the Rabbi so he might hold us, and sway, and let his head fall gently on our shoulder. So he might close his eyes and whisper our name in our ear. But the Rabbi and Beautiful Leonora are oblivious to our desires. They just keep dancing. It's as if we're not even really here.

I unfollow the Rabbi. I unfollow everything.

Two days later I long to follow something again. I look for the Rabbi, but he's gone. I don't see Beautiful Leonora either. If my friends still exist, their names have been changed. I try to follow Where Am I and I'm Sorry and I Do Not Wish to Burst Into Smithereens but no one is accepting new followers. It is freezing cold. And all the lights in this city are out. I turn around. My Husband and My Babies are following me. They are shivering. They turn around. I follow them. I turn around. They follow me. They turn around. I follow them. We are like toy soldiers patrolling a castle. It is so cold. We are turning blue. We are hungry. I put My Husband and My Babies on my back and carry them through the dark city. I search for the Rabbi everywhere. I search for Beautiful Leonora. I search for my friends. Like an animal, I howl for them. My Husband and My Babies are so heavy. Who will feed us? Who will keep us warm? How am I supposed to know where to go?

CLAY

In my day / Son / everybody knew how to pronounce
the word "faucet" / and everybody knew how to apolo-
gize / profusely, and everybody knew how to vanish. /
And when a man / drove up to your house with a truck
/ full of soil, mulch, and rocks / you knew he was there
to grow something, Son. He was there / to make a difference. Nowadays the world's so heavy / that very same
man is face / down in the flowers. Go try to talk to him,
Son. Go try and pick him up. He'll never rise / Unlike
the lonesome crowd in my heart that rose / and rose and
rose / to its feet when you arrived / cheering wildly, he'll
never rise / He'll never rise no matter how much green
fuzz from your green fuzzy mittens you flick at him / for

he is sour bones. / For it is my doom you undo / not his. For winter is here forever, Son, so bundle up. Here is your pancake / in the shape of a chicken. I'm sorry. I couldn't get the feathers / right. For a long time, Son, I pursued / happiness. I gave lectures on margins / and darkness. And when a hand / went up, and mouths would move, / sometimes I saw clouds. Sometimes even a little bit / of rain. But mostly nothing. And there you were far / in the back. In the very last row. There you were the whole / time, no not the whole time, but here you are now / with your clay, your colored clay. What are you making, Son? / An invisible ocean robot bird from Outer Space? Well that's as good / a thing as any. In my day, the war was off. / Nowadays, the war is super / on. I look around at what is left of us and wonder / where does all this love / come from? In my day, Son, we knew. The love / it came from the river called Mother or Hands or God or Some-thing. I do not know / why today of all days / I chose to wear this lemon yellow blouse. It fits me / terribly. "My words," you say / "are forgetting me." Me too, Son. Me too. Hold my hand. / It's a long walk home. / In my day, Son, it felt good / to lose everything. It felt like winning. /

And in my day, Son, laughter was fragile. You prayed /
for laughter, Son, and sometimes laughter / would never
come. And sometimes the joke / was on you and it was
heavy / and you were face down right beside the man /
face down in the flowers but you got up, Son. / In my
day, you got the hell up. / My throat is sore. My throat
has been sore / for a long, long time. You see that tree,
Son? It's a ghost. / It's all ghosts. I'm a ghost. / And you're
a ghost. This whole town / is a ghost. In my day, we all
knew / how to be ghosts. It meant / something to be a
ghost. And if your mother / was a ghost you were proud
/ of your mother. Nowadays, Son / all I ever want to do
is fix something. Something big. / Something incredibly
broken. When I was a little girl / I rocked back and forth
and sang the Hallelujah / in a dark wool dress. / In a big,
loud voice. / Nowadays, no one knows / how to apolo-
gize. No one knows how to vanish. / I'm trying to teach
you something, Son / about perseverance and grief and
forgiveness. You are almost four / and you want to stay
three / forever. "I don't want to be a very old man" / you
say, "with very white hair." Don't be frightened, Son. /
Everything is far away. / I was wrong. The man / in the

flowers is looking around. He is rising up. / Maybe he
would like to share / your colored clay? I'm sorry, Son /
I'm just a poet. I hope this is enough. / If it isn't I'll burn
down the house / and give you the ashes.

MY BROTHER GARY MADE A MOVIE & THIS IS WHAT HAPPENED

Although he is wearing a paper bag over his head, I instantly recognize Gary. Gary is my brother, and he is making a movie. Don't get me wrong, the eyes were cut out. I mean, Gary could *see*. "What's the name of the movie, Gary?" "The name of the moobie," said Gary, "is *My Family*." "You said moobie, Gary." "No, I didn't. I said, moobie." "You did it again, Gary."

Gary's eyes moved very quickly back and forth. Gary was miffed. "I'm going to flip out!" shouted Gary. "I'm sorry, Gary." Gary had trouble with words. It was his sorest spot. Sometimes he was so tragically far off I wanted to gather him up in my arms, climb a tree, and leave him in the largest nest I could find. He'd mean to say "human" and it would come out "cantaloupe." He'd mean to say "dad" and it would come out "sock." Even my name he malapropped. He called me Mouse.

"Did you build that camera yourself, Gary?" The camera was an old tin can with a bunch of leaves pasted to it. Gary held the tin can up in the air. A few leaves fluttered off. "Action?" he whispered. And then, even softer, he whispered, "Cut?" "May I make a suggestion, Gary?" "What is it, Mouse?" "Maybe you want to point the camera at something." "Like what?" "Maybe like an actor, Gary. Like an actor who is saying words." "Like these actors?" asked Gary. I was proud of his pronunciation. He led me behind the couch.

The actors groaned in a heap. "Is that Grandpa, Gary?" It was unquestionably Grandpa. He was on the very, very tippy top. "Hi, Grandpa," I said. "Hello," said Grandpa. He was not excited to see me. I had married a black man, and he was still ticked off. "This is not about you," said Grandpa. "This is about Gary and his burden of dreams."

"Look!" said Gary. "There's sock." Gary meant our dad. "Hi, Dad." My father gave a little wave. He was about four actors from the bottom. My eleven other brothers also were there: Eugene, Jack, Sid, Benjamin, Daniel, Saul, Eli, Walter, Adam, Richard, and Gus. They groaned. Aunt Rosa was shoved between my mother and grandmother. A bunch of cousins were balled up at the bottom.

"Hand me that shovel," said Gary. "What shovel?" I asked. But Gary already was pointing his tin can straight at the heap. "Lights," said Gary. "Turn off the lights!" I turned off the lights. "Camera," said Gary. "Action," said Gary. "Cut," said Gary.

"May I ask a question, Gary?" "What is it, Mouse?" "Why are you shooting in the dark, Gary?"

"I've had it," yelled my mother. "We've been here for six goddamn years." Aunt Rosa made little clucking sounds. I turned on the lights. Gary went into the kitchen and returned with a large tray filled with tiny cups of water.

"I can't live in a heap this close to your father," yelled my mother.

I began to wonder about footage.

"I need a mani/pedi," yelled my mother. "I need a god-damn blowout." "You look beautiful," I said. "This is not about you," yelled my mother. "This is about Gary and his burden of dreams." I handed her a cup of water. "This water tastes fake," yelled my mother. "It is fake," said Gary.

My father's beeper went off. His patients were dying.

"Did you know," asked Grandma, "that the fear of being touched is called aphenphosmphobia?" My mother rolled her eyes.

"What's the movie about, Gary?" "The moobie's about the Holocaust," said Gary.

"Is there a script, Gary?" "Bring me that ladder," said Gary. I brought him the ladder. He leaned it against the heap, climbed all the way up, and stood on top of Grandpa. Grandpa smiled.

Gary pulled the paper bag off his head. His silver hair tumbled out. The actors oohed and aahed. Gary blushed. He turned the paper bag inside out, and off of it he read the script: *Thou shalt have no other gods; Thou shalt not make any graven images; Thou shalt not take the Lord's name in vain; Remember the Sabbath day; Honor thy father and mother; Thou shalt not kill; Thou shalt not commit adultery; Thou shalt not steal; Thou shalt not bear false witness against thy neighbor; Thou shalt not covet thy neighbor's house . . . nor anything that is his.*

"Such a good boy," said Aunt Rosa. "Such a good boy," said Grandpa. "Such a good boy," said my father. "Go to hell," said my mother. My eleven other brothers groaned.

"Did you know," said Grandma, "that the fear of the skins of animals is called doraphobia?"

I began to wonder whose heart was a doomed spoon.
Mine or Gary's.

The best I could do for Gary at this point was hold him
and ask him what he was going to do after.

"After what?" asked Gary. "After shooting," I said. "I'm going to Barcelona," said Gary. Now that really ceiled me.
I would've said "that really threw me off the heap," but I
wasn't invited to be on the heap. Wasn't really sure I ever
wanted to be on the heap. "There are these scrambled eggs
in Barcelona," said Gary, "I really need to try." "Oh come
on, Gary. You know you'll scream the whole way." In the
States, Gary was just fussy. Overseas he screamed.

And then I remembered Gary's problem with mal-
apropping. "Barcelona?" I asked. "Barcelona," said Gary.
"Scrambled eggs?" I asked. "Scrambled eggs," said Gary.
I looked over at the heap. My mother was halfway out
of there. "Six more years," she yelled, "and then I quit."
My father gave Gary an idealistic thumbs up. "Did you
know," said Grandma, "that the fear of puppets is called

pupaphobia?" "Well," said Grandpa, "bye." "I'm not going yet," I said. I was still holding Gary. I held him as tightly as I hold my breath when I pass the cemetery. "Why do you do that?" asked Gary. "Do what?" "Hold your breath when you pass the cemetery?" I looked over at the heap. Aunt Rosa smacked her hand over her mouth to muffle her laughter, but she wasn't even laughing. She wasn't even smiling. "Because I don't," I whispered, "want to make the ghosts jealous." "This isn't about you," said Gary. "This is about me and my burden of dreams." "I know, Gary." "I know you know," said Gary. He picked a few leaves off the tin can and handed them to me. I put them in my mouth, chewed, and swallowed. A month later I was pregnant.

I stayed on the set until my husband, the black man, came to pick me up.

EVERYTHING WAS BEAUTIFUL
AND NOTHING HURT

"If you love Poems so much," says the bully, "why don't you marry Poems?" I have wandered onto a playground, accidentally. I am a sixty-seven-year-old woman standing on the 3 of a hopscotch game blurred by last night's rain. It is September. The swings smile their black rubberish smiles. I smile back, politely. "What's your name, Bully?" Bully puffs out his chest. "Beadlebaum," he says. "Listen, Beadlebaum, I did marry Poems. We've been married for years."

There is a space between Beadlebaum's front teeth that reminds me of Poems.

My cell rings. It's Ma. I tell her about the bully. I tell her his name is Beadlebaum and that the space between his front teeth reminds me of Poems. "Describe," says Ma. "Like wild shade," I say. "More," says Ma. "Like an empty Bible," I say. "How's that?" asks Ma. "Like if the Bible was a room you could walk inside and there was nothing. No Genesis, no Exodus, no Numbers, no god. No light, no darkness." Ma is silent. Beadlebaum coughs. "I don't really know," I say. "Stick with the shade," says Ma.

Beadlebaum's fists are clenched. He jumps and sways around me. He is shouting. "If you love Poems so much, why don't you marry Poems?" Beadlebaum is a bad listener. I crouch down and look Beadlebaum straight in the eye. I do not like repeating myself, but this time I do. I must. "I did marry Poems." For proof, I flash my band. Beadlebaum squints. "And not only did I marry Poems, but at the time we married it was only legal to do so in six states. We married in Iowa, Beadlebaum. Iowa. Have you ever believed, Beadlebaum, in something much, much bigger than you?" Beadlebaum is sweating. "Liar!" shouts Beadlebaum.

"Listen, Beadlebaum. It's a bad economy. You are trying to spend me when I've already been spent." I sit him on a bench and tie his shoelaces. "Some would say we're in a depression, Beadlebaum. Over the years I applied for dozens and dozens of jobs. I killed many interviews. Slaughtered them, in fact. I held those who may be concerned to my bosom and answered their questions so expertly I left them weeping. Weeping into my skin, Beadlebaum. Was I sloppy at times? Perhaps. Was my perfume magnificent? It was. Was I overly prepared? Never. Did they call me back, Beadlebaum? No, they did not. No one was really hiring. And if they were hiring they weren't paying. And if they were paying they were only paying Donald. Do you know Donald, Beadlebaum?" Beadlebaum shakes his head no. "Do you know why you don't know Donald? You don't know Donald because nobody knows Donald. Donald doesn't exist. Donald is the man none of us will ever be."

I peel Beadlebaum a hard-boiled egg and offer it to him. He turns his face away.

"I took courses on miracles, Beadlebaum. Honest to god miracles. And where did that leave me? Where did that leave me, Beadlebaum? I am asking you, Beadlebaum." Beadlebaum looks at me and blinks. "Where did taking courses on miracles leave me?"

"It left you on the playground with me?" "That's right, Beadlebaum. It left me on the playground with you."

Ma calls. "Do you need milk?" She is shouting. She thinks I am always in need of milk. "Not now, Ma," I say. "I am getting somewhere."

"The job market is an empty mouse. You know what that means, Beadlebaum?" Beadlebaum shakes his head no. "It means no blood. No bones. Not even a liver, Beadlebaum. Not even a couple of guts. It means just a sad pile of fur you couldn't, no matter how hard you tried, ever turn into a coat. Not even a lousy scarf, Beadlebaum. Nothing holds it together, Beadlebaum. Nothing holds it together." Beadlebaum looks like he's about to cry. I muss his hair, as Ma once mussed mine.

Up and down the seesaw we go.

"Have you ever put on a suit, Beadlebaum? Have you ever showed up exactly on time with hope in your heart? Have you ever been the most qualified candidate, by far?" Beadlebaum looks down at his skinny hands. Beadlebaum tries to run away, but I catch him by the collar.

Poems is looking for me. Sometimes I get lost, like today.

Ma calls. She tells me she is reading *Slaughterhouse-Five*. "It says here," says Ma, "EVERYTHING WAS BEAUTIFUL AND NOTHING HURT." She says this to reassure me. As if she's reading the newspaper, and not a drawing of a gravestone in a book. Ma's sharp, but lousy with fiction. Beadlebaum holds my hand. We watch the toads hop across the damp ground. "They know something we don't know," says Beadlebaum. And they do. The toads do.

Just when I begin to wonder if Beadlebaum is a real child, Poems shows up. Beautiful Poems, the color of upturned soil.

Poems walks straight up to Beadlebaum. "There's a new sheriff in town," he says. But Poems doesn't say this like a sheriff. He doesn't say this like he's protecting me. He says this like he's missing. In a whisper.

He feels for the badge on his chest but there is no badge. "Maybe it dropped," says Beadlebaum. They are on their hands and knees. They are looking for the badge so Poems can show Beadlebaum he's the new sheriff in town. They crawl under the monkey bars. "It's gold and star shaped," says Poems. "I know," says Beadlebaum.

"Everybody knows that," says Beadlebaum. "Even babies. Even," Beadlebaum says pointing at me, "her." Then he picks up a rock and throws it at my head. There is blood. "If you love Poems so much why don't you marry Poems?" Poems looks distraught.

"Do the thing," says Beadlebaum, "where you cry." And Poems cries.

Poems cries so hard a cloud bursts, and children spill out. They fall through the air. Their legs and arms go in every direction like sunshine. They land softly. They flood the playground in brightly colored pajamas.

They are carrying books, keys, bones, the bareness of my being. Some are carrying each other. They march up to Beadlebaum and surround him. Of all the children, Beadlebaum seems the most elderly. Pale Beadlebaum. In his fake-corduroy shorts.

Ma calls. "There is no such thing as fake corduroy," says Ma. "Only corduroy, regular. It's like skin," says Ma. "It's either skin or if it's fake it's something else."

Now Beadlebaum is in the middle of a thick circle of children who have fallen from the clouds. They do not taunt him or throw bones. They just stare and hum and ask Beadlebaum who he loves. "Who do you love, Beadlebaum?"

Ma calls. "It's impolite to love no one," she says. And Ma would know. I tell Ma my head is bleeding. "Of course it is," says Ma.

Poems is on the swings crying and crying. Clouds are bursting with more and more children. "Beadlebaum, Beadlebaum, who do you love?" The children are singing. The children are swaying. And then Beadlebaum's voice. Muffled by all the children, but I know it's Beadlebaum in there. "Beadlebaum, Beadlebaum, who do you love?" I hear it, and just when I hear it, just when I hear Beadlebaum say my name, Poems is beside me. Poems has collected some leaves to wipe the blood from my head. I tell Poems it's me. I tell Poems Beadlebaum loves me. But then I hear Beadlebaum say "Poland." Then I hear Beadlebaum say "fish." Then Beadlebaum says "nose." Poems is wiping away all the blood. I close my eyes. I tell Poems Beadlebaum said my name. Poems says, "Shhhh." Ma is calling. I hear Beadlebaum say, "forgive." There is so much blood. This is how Poems saves me.

MOTHER AT THE DENTIST

Every day, for the past ten years, my mother calls me from the dentist. "Can you believe I am here?" she asks. "*Again!*" And I can. There are so many teeth. There is a lot of work on my mother's mouth to do, and Dr. Fishman is the best. My father has moved on. A man can only wait for his wife at the dentist for so long until he wanders outside to buy a newspaper and never returns. "Barbara!" She is yelling. "Are you there?" And I am. I am there. "I really wish you'd get married already," she sighs. She sounds like her mouth is slowly filling up with mice. "Maybe it would help if you cut out the sugar." I look around. There is no sugar. Whether there had ever been any sugar, I can barely remember. In the distance, there is drilling, but

I can't tell if it's coming from my mother's end or mine. "Barbara! Are you listening? Just between you and me this Dr. Fishman is a nudnick! He's a louse! A thief!" She says this romantically. "I am never coming back." But she will come back. She will come back every day. She loves Dr. Fishman almost as much as he loves her. "If I die here, Barbara, you can have all my jewelry." I look around my bare apartment. My mother still has all her baby teeth. She refuses to let them fall out. She calls them Mindy, and I suspect Dr. Fishman has no choice but to call them Mindy too. I have watched her pet them with her tongue, and grown jealous.

The next day, my mother calls me from the dentist. "Can you believe I am here?" she asks. "*Again!*" And I can. There are so many teeth. "He wants to give me a crown," she giggles. "Like a princess." There is the fuzzy sound of what may be Dr. Fishman's beard brushing up against the phone. "He promises to build me a bridge," she coos. "Like in the movies." I don't know what to say so I ask my mother what her favorite color is. But my mother can't hear me, or can't answer, or doesn't want to. She puts Dr.

Fishman on the phone. "Of course your mother loves you, Barbara. Don't be ridiculous. It's your choices she doesn't love. I am handing you back to your mother." I can hear my mother ask who it is. "It's Barbara." There's a long silence. Then scraping. Then I hear kissing noises. Then more silence. Then "Barbara!" She is yelling. "Are you there?" And I am. I am there. "It's moss," she says. "My favorite color is moss." She is not being serious. No one's favorite color is moss, least of all my mother's.

At night, as I try to fall asleep, I wonder about Dr. Fishman's other patients. All dusty and still in the waiting room.

The next day, my mother calls me from the dentist. "Can you believe I am here?" she asks. "*Again!*" And I can. There are so many teeth. "Remember, Barbara, when you were ten and I took you to the swamp?" My mother never took me to a swamp. "Remember the boats, Barbara? Remember the mosquitoes?" My mother is laughing. I can hear Dr. Fishman laughing too. My mother covers the phone, but I can still hear everything. "I took her to the swamp, and she tried to drink the water." My mother gargles, then

MOTHER AT THE DENTIST

spits. "Talk about your swamp faux pas!" Now my mother and Dr. Fishman are growling with laughter. "Why were you so thirsty, Barbara?" She doesn't wait for me to answer. She covers the phone again, but I can still hear her. "She made tiny paper hats for the frogs, and taped balloons to the trees. Can you imagine!" More laughter. "Why can't you ever just let a swamp be a swamp, Barbara? Why do you always have to fight against nature?" My mother never took me to a swamp. I have never, not once in my life, fought against nature. I am beginning to wonder if she's thinking not of a swamp, but of my tenth birthday. "Barbara, Barbara, are you there?" Now it's Dr. Fishman on the phone. "Your mother, you should know, has gorgeous breath." Dr. Fishman says this as if he's disappointed in me.

The next day, my mother calls me from the dentist. "Can you believe I am here?" she asks. "*Again!*" And I can. There are so many teeth. "I am worried about your lack of gumption, Barbara. Where'd you leave it, Barbara? Where's your get up and go?" Before I can explain I can't get up and go because who would answer her calls from the dentist, she starts up again about my gumption. "I am worried, Barbara, about your gumption." My mother keeps repeating gumption like she's sucking on a sour candy. "Dr. Fishman agrees with me, Barbara. You are seriously lacking gumption. Where is it, Barbara? Where's your gumption, Barbara? Where are your gums, Barbara? Where are your gummy, gum, gums?" I run my finger across my gums. Upper and lower. They're still there, but barely. "Did the wolf get them, Barbara? Did he huff and puff and blow them all down?"

The next day, my mother calls me from the dentist. "Can you believe I am here?" she asks. She sounds less certain, smaller. "*Again*?" she whispers. And I can. There are so many teeth. My mother goes silent. I wait. Something is different. "No one is here," she says. She sounds terrified. "Can I come over?" I want to say yes, but I say no. If my mother has taught me anything it's to change nothing. There is a knock on my door. It's too soon to be my mother. I look through the peephole. There is a crowd of men, women, and children. They are holding rolled up magazines. Their mouths are wide open.

FOR THE SAFETY
OF OUR COUNTRY

Today is a new batch. The Presidents come from all over. Perishable Presidents in thinning sweaters. Presidents bent like moons. Thirsty Presidents. Humming Presidents. Thick, winterish Presidents. Sick Presidents. Beautiful Presidents. See-through Presidents. Watery Presidents. Presidents with faces blank as almonds. Hollering Presidents. Sad Presidents. Sadder Presidents. Presidents skinny as twigs. Presidents soft as bread. "We're here," announces the bus driver, "White House." The Presidents stumble off the old yellow bus that was once, long ago, used for schoolchildren. "We're lost?" asks one President, squinting in the sunlight. "Not yet," says another. "More like we're becoming lost." I'm the one in charge. I am small, but quick. And I'm a hard worker. As they de-

46

scend, I hand each President a sack lunch of chicken legs and oranges. I hand each President a small bottle of water. "Nobody is lost," I assure them. "See," I say, spreading my arms wide enough to hug them all, "we're all right here."

As they walk toward me, they leave behind like uprooted trees the barest trace of earth.

None of the Presidents smile.

They go through the turnstiles. Entrance is free.

I come from a long line of superstitious people. We spit three times, we keep salt in our pockets, we wear tiny hands against our chests, we throw no baby showers, we chew on thread, we break the glass, we knock on wood, we rarely smile for fear of bringing attention to a happiness we rarely feel, for fear of someone out of nowhere taking our happiness away. And so I don't expect anything from the Presidents. I barely expect them to stay alive. And this, for all of us, is a relief. This is why they put me in charge.

Yesterday I sent the last batch along their merry way. No

one was whistling, least of all me. Like charred paper up a chimney, the old Presidents were here and then they were gone.

The new Presidents fan out on the grounds that are lush because of me. They shyly peel the meat away from the bone and eat. They chew stiffly. The grass on these greens is greener than most greens are green, and wilder. Some Presidents get caught in the thicket and copse, but I untangle them before they even know it.

When they are done with lunch, I show the Presidents around. "Here is the dark pond. Here is the rec room, the china room, the crying room. Here is the library and here is the secret library. Here is the water fountain, but it doesn't work. It never worked. And over there," I point to over there, "is where the nickels and dimes are kept. And over there are all the pennies."

"And here are your beds." Thirteen rows of beds, like stripes on a flag. "One bed per President," I instruct. "Don't take two beds, because you only need one." A few Presidents twist and mat together like fur, but I comb them out. I want to ask the Presidents if they remember animals but I know now isn't the time. It's never really the time. "At the Eleventh Hour," I announce, "we'll meet back at the rec room." "What?" asks a President. "At the Eleventh Hour," I say as loudly as I can, "we'll meet back at the rec room." The Presidents will forget. They are still busy choosing beds. I will remind them twice more.

Among the Presidents there is one President named Huh. I notice him immediately. His black coat is soft and frayed. If in his graying beard is one half-written poem folded up many times, I won't be surprised at all. He picks his bed last. I linger, though I shouldn't, as he opens his suitcase. Nothing but dustpans. He stacks them carefully beside his bed. He sees me seeing. Dustpans. It's unquestionably a hearty collection.

Something about Huh makes me want to throw a stone into the sea, but there is no sea anymore. And the stones were collected and hauled away years ago.

It's against the rules for me to love one President more than another.

I slip away down the hall. A bouquet of Presidents. I pull them apart at the neck. This is part of my job. Unbunching.

I spray windex on our motto: "You Are Here for the Safety of Our Country." I wipe it until it shines. I mop the floors with something scentless. I pick up everything the Presidents drop: pencils, socks, candy wrappers, loose leaf paper, apple peels, toothbrushes, dollar bills, bars of soap, postage stamps, worry dolls, shoelaces, combs, buttons, receipts, nail clippers, sometimes even a tooth. Soon it will be the Eleventh Hour. I go to my room to change into something more significant.

The President named Huh knocks on my door. "What's this country's name again?" I tell him the name. "See," says Huh, "it has no ring to it." He leads me to the window. "Look," he says. "All these people in their colorful T-shirts just staring up at me all day. It's too much. I mean, I'm just a man." I look out the window. There is no one there. There hasn't been anyone there for years. He looks off into the distance. "How do you spell 'Woo Hoo'?" "Some people," I say, "use a dash. But I like it without." He reaches into his pocket and pulls out a wishbone. We crack it. He gets the larger piece, closes his eyes, and makes what looks like a wish. "What did you wish?" I ask. The terrain on Huh's face is silent, still. "I wished for nothing. I'm just a man," he says. "And this is just a country." He looks back out the window. "And those are just citizens." I look carefully through the glass. There is no one there. "There's nothing to wish for," says Huh. He takes my hand and leads me back to his dustpans. "And those are just dustpans." I look at the dustpans. It really is a hearty collection. I notice his breath: paltry. Puny. Under his left eye appears to be a small patch of moss where a flower could grow if only he believed in himself a little more.

Huh and I stand beside his bed holding hands for a long time. It's impossible to tell one dustpan from another.

"At home," says Huh, "I used to keep sheep. But the sheep got distraught." "Of course they did," I say patting his back. Sadly he chuckles. He touches my thinning hair. I touch his beard hoping to find something, but it's empty. Not even a dustpan. Not even a small one. Huh goes back to his quarters, and I go back to mine.

When I arrive at the Eleventh Hour the Presidents are already drinking fruit punch out of small paper cups. Traces of pink mustaches float above their lips. The orange and blue and red and yellow and purple crepe streamers suggest a celebration. A knot of Presidents thickens behind me. I loosen them. I see Huh. He has the look of a man who left his only son, one hundred years ago, on a windowsill. Frantic and defeated. I go to Huh. I have to fight a little through the streamers to get to him, but I get to him. "Something happened," says Huh. His lips are dusty. "Something is always happening," I say. The Presidents, like water, swell around Huh. I look into their eyes. Cracked seashells. They've been through so much. "You've been through so much," I say. The Presidents nod. The Presidents turn their pockets and out spill crushed flowers they've picked for no one. The Presidents' heads are bent, and they are making little gray sounds. Sometimes I look at the Presidents and dream of another life.

The Presidents have done nothing wrong. Not really.

"Something happened," says Huh again. "We've been briefed." "The trees," says a President, "have been shot." "Which trees," I ask, though I know. "The Aleppo trees," says a President. "The Aleppo trees have been shot," says a President. "What does Aleppo mean?" asks a President. "It means to give milk to travelers as they pass through the region," says a President. "Oh," says a President. "Milk," says a President. "Trees," says a President. "Region," says a President. "Do we need Aleppo trees?" asks a President. "On that we haven't yet been briefed." "Have all the trees been shot?" asks a President. "Most of them," says a President. "And what fruit do they bear if they bear fruit at all?" asks a President. "Pear," says a President. "But rarely," says a President. "Rarer than rarely," says another. "Never," says another. I let the Presidents go on about the trees as I hand each President a white nightgown to change into before bed. "What should we do about the trees?" yawns a President. "Maybe we should tell them to just surren-der," suggests another. "It's getting late," I whisper like a mother. A thin layer of mildew has begun to grow over the Presidents' faces. I open a window. The Presidents' white nightgowns quiver, it seems, in the wind. But there is no wind anymore. So it cannot be the wind.

"The trees have been shot," says a President. "For their timber," says a President.

Some of the Presidents, like scattered hail, have already curled into small white balls and fallen soundly asleep.

The others drift silently into their beds, leaving behind a trail of pear seeds. Seeds from the fruit the Aleppo trees will never bear. I sweep up the pear seeds and the sound of my sweeping sounds like *for their timber, for their timber, for their timber.* Huh hands me a dustpan. Into it I sweep the seeds. There are so many seeds. Huh smiles. Between his teeth are seeds. His eyes are seeds. Caked in his fingernails are seeds.

"Tomorrow is another day," I say. Although it isn't really. For the Presidents there is only ever really one day. Huh climbs over his stack of dustpans and tucks himself in. I want to kiss Huh, but there are no kisses anymore. The kisses ended a long time ago too.

The Presidents breathe in and breathe out, in and out. I look out the window. In the distance very small bodies are dragging behind them very soft things. I close the curtains. The Presidents need their sleep.

Had January not ended a long time ago, in the morning it would've been the first day of January. And it might have rained had rain not ended. And there might have been the sound of children playing had children not ended. Soon everything will end. Soon the mountains will end. And the snow on the mountains will end. And the sunshine will end, and the moon will end. And soon the very, very last President will arrive and then Presidents will end too. And then it will just be me. The very last citizen. Standing quietly in the dark. Knowing I did everything I could to make this country a safer place.

SISTER

What the meaning of Sister is I am unable to say.

She and Mother rush past me on Broadway. In their furred hoods they are part of the same outfit. One sixty-three, the other twenty-four, they are having some kind of thin, dry happiness with each other. "Hi, Sister!" I call out. "Hi, Mom!" I am buying fruit. Mostly apples, occasionally a pear. "Who cares," snorts Sister. She is Mother's later, better daughter. They are already blocks away.

From Paris, Mother and Sister send postcards. One is of kneesocks. "What do you think of these kneesocks, Mumford? Aren't they so tart?" And they are. They are so tart. Though my name is Judy, Sister calls me Mumford. Now everyone calls me Mumford. Even my boyfriend who is missing calls me Mumford. Mother and Sister are so rich. I do not like the name Mumford. It sounds like the name you use if you don't have a name, which I do. It's Judy.

What is wrong with Sister is that frost gathers around her mouth even in summer.

Sister and Mother invite me out to dinner. When I arrive at the restaurant they are already bent over their menus. Also, they are singing. "Tinker, Tailor, Soldier, Sailor, Rich Man, Poor Man, Beggar Man, Thief." At "thief" they look up fast and point at me. They have clearly practiced this because it's perfectly performed. "No offense," snarls Sister. "None taken," I swallow. But I have taken offense. I have taken so much offense I can barely breathe. I can't imagine what I've stolen.

At the hospital, Sister and I wait for Mother's results. It appears Mother's body is out of water. The doctors slosh in and out of her room with jugs, pails, drums, buckets, et cetera. "She will be fixed by Friday," they promise. "Easy peasy." Sister is assured. She knows these doctors, personally. "The difference between me and you, Mumford, is that I have clout whereas you have no clout." At first I think Sister is saying clouds. That I have no clouds. "Where would mother be without my clouds?" yawns Sister. She blows kisses to the doctors. They giggle and swoon. Outside, the city is bursting with freedom.

When I finally show this Sister to our father he is genuinely surprised. Sister brushes crumbs off her designer sweater and nods hello. "Hello," says Dad. "Beautiful day." Sister looks at her watch. She squints up at our father as if he were a Greyhound bus in a sunlit parking lot. "No seats," she says. "Mumford," she says, "I am catastrophically bored. Get me out of here, Mum. Pick me up and carry me. I am too thick with ennui to walk." I pick up Sister. Her expensive legs dangle everywhere. Sister has never before allowed me to touch her. I feel like a hero. When I return Sister to Mother, Mother punches me in the face. And then Sister punches me in the face. And then Mother. And then Sister. And then Mother. And then Sister. In the distance, I can hear Dad whistling.

At the health club, Sister and Mother are on the elliptical. Their bodies swoosh. I stare up at their fitness. Today I am not even trying. I munch on snacks in a pleated skirt. "Haven't I grown," asks Sister, "so much as a person?" I nod. Mother beams. "As a person, Mumford, I have grown so much. As a person, have you? No, Mum, as a person you have not grown so much. In fact, you have grown not at all. Mumford, Mummelah, Mother got off so cheap with you, didn't you, Mother? Didn't you say so?" Mother nods. "You know why, Mums?" I shake my head no because I don't know why. "I will tell you why, Mumster. Mother got off so cheap because you loathe to ask for what you will never ever ever ever ever ever deserve. Furthermore, you lack imperturbability. You are overly perturbed. Come here, Mumford. Set your snacks down. Listen to me, Mumford. You are chubby and your boyfriend is missing forever. You are, and here I am only quoting Mother, a misery on Earth. Also, Mums, it is impossible to tell if you really love a mouse or if you only love the word 'mouse' for some exhausting reason. This makes you untrustworthy, Mumford. Which is it, Mumford? Mouse or 'mouse'? You are such a meanie, Mumford. I know you keep a mouse when all you really wish to keep is what it's called. Step aside, Mumford, your largeness is in all the trainers' way. Your long glances are too long. Your terribly written fables are filled with inoperative motifs. Everything you do, Mum, is so *unrealistic*. Let me tell you something, Mumford. Let me shed some light on why you are soused in a sadness that could've so easily been vanished had Mother doted on you for one second. It is because on you, and I hope I get this right, because on you she cannot dote. Isn't that right, Mother?" Mother nods. "About you she is lukewarm." Mother nods more. "Doting on you is impossible, Mumford. You are ugly, Mum. Even if I had one thousand sons none of them would ever be your nephew. Are you listening, Mumford? None of them would ever call you Aunt or Auntie or Aunt Mumford. Not even the worst of them. Are you listening, Mumford? Are you getting this? Or have you drifted off to sleep as you so often do? Try to get the gist of a barbell, Mumford. Maybe that will help, at the very least, your figure."

On the battlefield, Mother and Sister sneak out of view. I pick up Sister's gun. Hilarity does not ensue. Nothing, in fact, ensues. Aside from a sycamore, I stand alone. My scalp itches. Where is my insurgency? I look around. My insurgency is late. I long for swag, but I know no swag will come. I long for loot, but the loot is long gone. If I were Sister, I wonder, would I relish this time alone? If I were Sister, standing here, holding Sister's gun, would I be seized with a great feeling of greatness? If my skin, like the sycamore, flaked off in large patches, could there ever be a Sister underneath? Maybe not a whole, perfect Sister, but a little piece of Sister? Just a small, terrified piece of Sister bursting out of me? I hold Sister's gun up to my nose and slowly breathe in. It smells like nothing. I look around the empty battlefield. If only Sister and Mother had stayed. I really think they could've loved it here.

SPELLS

Some look like sesame seeds. Hard and flat and thin. Some like sharp snowflakes. Some like the teeth of salt if salt had teeth. Bring your children out into the sunlight. Part your children's hair. A louse is wingless. It lives about a quarter inch away from the scalp. The eggs hold on for dear life. Often they are the same color as the hair. I am explaining this to the mother over the telephone. The mother says she will be at my door in an hour. With the heads of her children that have been itching for days.

Before the endless rain, before my nine sons turned into nine daughters all at once, I was the Lice Lady. The town's only one. There were stories about my metal comb. My impeccable work. Although it is possible I was the best Lice Lady on Earth, no one to this day has sent me a letter of recognition. Nowhere have I been honored in a large room with chandeliers and steaks. But I did beautiful work. I would tell the child to sit still, melt a tablespoon of margarine, rub it all over the head, and then from crown to end go hair by hair, taking special care around the ears while the mother sat there pale and bereft. With a paper towel, I would wipe the lice from the comb, and like handwriting the lice would settle into the creases. I have the patience of the dead.

I even taught my sons how to comb. Before they turned into daughters all at once.

With infestation comes a shame that can pull even the richest off their high horse and knock them to the ground. And it is from this low place the mothers and the children come to me. I open the door. A thick little gray cloud, shaped like two hearts stuck together, hangs over our house. "Something is brewing," says the mother, looking up at the sky. She pushes her misty children toward me.

The taller one is holding a large loaf of bread. "Do as she says," says the mother. And they nod.

I comb in the kitchen where the light is best.

The boy with the bread sits perfectly still. I part and comb, part and comb. A piece of me already knows, when I wipe off the comb, and the dead lice spell out five of my sons' names, marking the paper towel like it is a birth certificate, that something terrible is about to happen. Each name perfectly spelled, perfectly legible. The boy with the bread looks straight ahead, never blinking. His sister is next. A stiff, quiet child. When she sits I hear her bones creak. What comes off her head are the rest of the names. The color of wheat and ash. A piece of me knew even before the lice. For days my sons' ears appeared to be softening, and I could already smell the mean lilac. The small crack on the kitchen ceiling, shaped like a hand, was spreading. I had heard of this happening. But not to nine sons at once unless they were all tucked away in cupboards by a stepmother with no name. Or maybe on a back road thick with sycamores. Or at the very top of an old hill. But not here. Here when I pull the metal comb through the hair the lice come with it. They don't turn into butterflies. They don't turn into sparrows or soot. Here trees live and die as trees.

The sky darkens, and I worry. It is almost five o'clock. It is almost time to wash my sons' feet, but I am still combing. The rain begins and the mother pays. My oldest son puts his hand on my shoulder. Soon I will love them all less.

After seven to ten days, the nit hatches and becomes what is known as a nymph, or a young louse. Cycles are essential to life. Without patterns our bodies would wander off into the middle of a parched field and just stand there staring up at the sky. And so everyday at five on the dot I wash my sons' feet. Nine sons. Eighteen feet. I go down the line with my bucket. The suds grow feathery between their toes. I slowly scrub their heels with a stone, releasing a small puff of dust. A sob. My sons' beautiful faces begin to blur and I know it is happening. I know it is about to happen. If they have to change into something maybe they will change into wild swans. Anything but daughters. The phone rings. A mother. Her children are scratching. She will come first thing in the morning. When I return it's too late. Instead of my sons, there is a spray of half-finished daughters, each holding her nose. Their legs extended. Their toes in the horrible air. "Ew, lice," bleats the oldest. Maybe goats, for a moment, I pray. Hooves, I pray. Anything but daughters. It's too late. They are coming into focus. They are all gigantic. And they are daughters. The soft smell of lavender soap goes sick, feverish. The air fills with the smell of dead fruit.

"Give them some sand in a teacup and tell them to pretend it is cake," says my husband. It is possible he has been here the whole time.

When I was a child, everyday I wore the same yellow, wool cardigan. It had a little rainbow patch to hide a hole on the left elbow. Each button was a different color star. Eventually, my body burst out of it leaving me without a childhood.

I don't like change and I don't like daughters.

And now here they are. Sleepy and dumb, like honey. They open their mouths and I shine a light down their throats, and it's just as I'd suspected. Nothing but wildflowers and grass. I would send out a search party, but what is lost is all here.

This is what I remember most about my sons: they were always thirsty, and they were wildest at dusk, and they were always kind. Their eyes were soft and bright like snowy windowsills.

Now I have these gigantic daughters eating up all the strawberries and staring at me, accusingly. I look out at the empty hills. My sons once, yesterday, ran up and down those hills. Dirt and twigs in their sweet curls. The largest daughter steps on my foot. She reminds me of a full, angry moon. Tomorrow is her birthday. And the next day is her birthday too.

I take a metal comb to their heads. The lice come out in thick batches.

I line them up from giant to giantest: #1 face of a pink eraser, #2 riddled with holes, #3 opening up a small brown package, #4 smells of flooding, #5 with a pencil she is drawing her sisters with no hands, #6 afraid, #7 asleep, #8 famished, #9 glares.

I am their mother.

The rain is getting heavier. In our living room is a leak. The daughters take turns standing under it, mouths open, until I replace them with a bucket.

The daughters are deeply infested. It will take me days, weeks, months to comb them all out. I cancel my appointments. "Melody," says a daughter. How does she know my name? "No," I say. "No."

For months and months I comb, but as soon as a head is clear it freshly blooms with new lice. "We are under a spell," whispers my husband. He shaves off his hair and stands in the cold bedroom. In the afternoons I watch him through the keyhole. The daughters have caused us to creep around each other, never touching. They cling to him. They chew on his sleeves.

I dream my sons return to me, floating through the kitchen with bundles of wood. They have returned to build a boat. My youngest son, as he saws, begins to sing. *Row, row, row your boat gently down the stream. Pregnantly, pregnantly, pregnantly, pregnantly life is but a dream.* One piece of wood is pocked with rows of tiny holes I can't stop licking. I don't know what I'm doing with the wood. I sand and carve and saw. I lick and I lick. "Don't worry," says a son. "This is the part that doesn't matter."

I wake up with a horrible headache. My husband hands me a fistful of pebbles and I swallow them all.

My husband and I display ourselves to the daughters at dinner. We stand side by side. We do not quarrel. Peace is what pain looks like in public.

I give the daughters a head of lettuce. A faint smile slowly spreads over their mouths. Like a baby snake crawling over white, boring sand. They tear the leaves from the head and eat.

Inside the walls it is raining. Inside my husband it is raining. Lice can survive under water for several hours by holding their breath. Puddles quickly begin to dot the house. A small puddle forms under each daughter. The floorboards swell.

I crawl beneath my bed. They are always looking for me. "What are your names?" I finally ask. "Alice." And then the next one says "Alice" too. They are all named Alice. It's unbearable. They sit in the puddles, heavy-lidded.

Lice favor the nape of the neck and behind the ears. A louse will die within one to two days off its host.

I hate these daughters. When they appear to me again their heads are shaved and they are wearing little golden crowns. "Where did you get the crowns?" I ask. "From Papa," they swoon. My husband laughs little yellow stained laughs. And then the Alices laugh little yellow stained laughs too. It's so disgusting. "Go out into the world and get your own living." But they cannot go out. Our house is surrounded by water. Our streets have turned to rivers. My sons are gone and not once did a single trumpet cry out. Not once. Out of paper, I fold a boat. And then I fold another, and then another. But they're crooked and torn. Like a single misshapen body the Alices try to climb into one. "That's not your boat," I say, crumpling it up. With a broom I shoo them all away.

Now that their heads are shaved, the lice find other spots. I watch the Alices pull lice out of each other's knees. They leave the bodies in a bowl beside my bed.

My metal comb rusts. My fingers are dotted with mold.

Damp and cold from endless rain, the daughters huddle like nine enormous hard-boiled eggs, peeled and crowded in a bowl. Without my sons, my fingers grow long and shriveled. I miss my sons and all the air once between them, crisp like split pine. I miss their handsome faces. I cannot breathe. My nose hooks. My feet curl and root. My husband reaches for me, but I'm more tree than woman. My limbs are old, mean branches. Occasionally a lost flower blossoms on my hand, but quickly withers and drops to the ground. A daughter shoves it in her mouth. Every single time. The house is filling up with water. One foot high and rising.

It took me years, but if you listen very carefully you can hear the lice. They go *tick tock, tick tock, tick tock.* Their stories are thin and dark. For the last few days all they've said is "mother," over and over again as the daughters thickened into a fog.

But now they finally begin to tell me this story.

"Even if we wanted to," it begins, "where would we go? There is nowhere to go. We sleep on the roof now. Until the water carries us away."

My husband and daughters touch my bark. I stand very still. Soon they will chop me down and use my body to save themselves. A log to hold onto. A Melody to row them all the hell away.

THE VERY NERVOUS FAMILY

Mr. Horowitz clutches a bag of dried apricots to his chest. Although the sun is shining, there will probably be a storm. Electricity will be lost. Possibly forever. When this happens the very nervous family will be the last to starve. Because of the apricots. "Unless," says Mrs. Horowitz, "the authorities confiscate the apricots." Mr. Horowitz clutches the bag of dried apricots tighter. He should've bought two bags. One for the authorities and one for his very nervous family. Mrs. Horowitz would dead bolt the front door to keep the authorities out, but it is already bolted. Already dead. She doesn't like that phrase. Dead bolt. It reminds her of getting shot before you even have a chance to run. "Everyone should have at least a *chance* to run," says Mrs. Horowitz. "Don't you agree, Mr. Horowitz?" Mrs.

Horowitz always refers to her husband as Mr. Horowitz, should they ever one day become strangers to each other. Mr. Horowitz agrees. When the authorities come they should give the Horowitzs a chance to run before they shoot them for the apricots. Eli Horowitz, their very nervous son, rushes in with his knitting. "Do not rush," says Mr. Horowitz, "you will fall and you will die." Eli wants ice skates for his birthday. "We are not a family who ice skates!" shouts Mrs. Horowitz. She is not angry. She is a mother who simply does not wish to outlive her only son. Mrs. Horowitz gathers her very nervous son in her arms, and gently explains that families who ice skate become the ice they slip on. The cracks they fall through. The frost that bites them. "We have survived this long to become our own demise?" asks Mrs. Horowitz. "No," whispers Eli, "we have not." Mr. Horowitz removes one dried apricot from the bag and nervously begins to pet it when Mrs. Horowitz suddenly gasps. She thinks she may have forgotten to buy milk. Without milk they will choke on the apricots. Eli rushes to the freezer with his knitting. There is milk. The whole freezer is stuffed with milk. Eli removes a frozen half pint and glides it across the kitchen table. It is like the milk is skating. He wishes he were milk. Brave milk. He throws the half pint on the floor and stomps on it. Now the milk is crushed. Now the milk is dead. Now the Horowitzs are that much closer to choking. Mr. and Mrs. Horowitz are dumbfounded. Their very nervous son might be a maniac. He is eight. God is punishing them for being survivors. God has given them a maniac for a son. All they ask is that they not starve, and now their only son is killing milk. Who will marry their maniac? No one. Who will mother their grandchildren? There will be no grandchildren. All they ask is that there is something left of them when they are shot for the apricots, but now their only son is a maniac who will give them no grandchildren. Mr. Horowitz considers leaving Eli behind when he and Mrs. Horowitz run for their lives.

POOL

Jump into the pool, says Brother.

I do not wish to jump into the pool.
For old time's sake, says Brother, jump into the pool.
This pool looks different from the pool of yesteryear.
Make a splash, says Brother. Set an example for all the merry children lining up behind you, says Brother.
I turn around. These children do not look merry. They look very unmerry. Unmerry as fossils.
Jump into the pool, says Brother.
I do not wish to jump into the pool. There is a tree in the pool.
That is not a tree. That is Grandmother.

Grandmother, is that you?

No answer.

She is in the deep end trying to be misteriosa, says Brother.

I can assure you that tree is not a tree but Grandmother, backstroking.

More children are lining up behind me. Some appear to be geniuses.

Dip the big toe first and the body will come along after, says Brother.

How soon along after?

Depends, says Brother. A day at most.

Is there a plethora of ways? I ask.

There is a plethora.

Go on, I say.

You can *jump* into the pool, suggests Brother.

Go on, I say.

Or you could jackknife, bellyflop, pencil drop, cannonball, face the music, live the life, knuckle the mouse, happy-go-lucky, bury the hatchet, or hubba hubba.

Or I could sink, I say.

Or you could sink, says Brother.

Grandmother? No answer. Grandmother, is that you? No answer.

I do not like this pool.

I point north. Would it be possible to jump into that pool? Brother squints.

Brother scratches his head.

It seems to be a better pool.

From faraway, agrees Brother, it does seem to be a better pool.

A much better pool.

Loads better, says Brother.

I turn around. There appear to be hundreds of children lining up behind me, possibly thousands.

Jump into this pool, says Brother. Afterwards, you can have a snack at the snack bar.

I have been to that snack bar. It is a hideous snack bar.

It is a very hideous snack bar, agrees Brother.

I know no snack bar more hideous.

Any snack bar anywhere would be less hideous.

The popsicles are gaunt.

Impossibly gaunt, agrees Brother.

Grandmother floats by.

I am going to die soon, sings Grandmother.

I do not know that song.

Nor do I, says Brother.

Jump into the pool, says Brother.

Don't look, I say.

They're here, I say.

Who? asks Brother.

Our parents.

Where? whispers Brother.

At the end of the line.

They are younger than they should be, says Brother.

They appear to be teenagers.

They are very beautiful, says Brother.

Remarkably beautiful, I agree.

Mother is holding a hot pink inflatable ball.

Father is laughing.

Their intention is to jump into the pool and play.

Little do they know, says Brother.

Little do they know! cheer the children.

Little do they know, sighs Grandmother.

Jump into the pool, says Brother.

Hurry up, says Brother, it is time.
Some of the children, from the heat, are drying up.
It's a cruel world, says Brother.
There is no world more cruel, I say.
A crueler world, says Brother, there isn't.
Do you know Gloria? asks Brother.
I do not know Gloria.
Suddenly I find myself in love with Gloria, says Brother.
I must go to her, says Brother.
If you go to Gloria who will tell me to jump into the pool?
Brother thinks.
Grandmother floats by.
Brother thinks more.
Our parents are too far back.
No one, says Brother. If I go to Gloria, no one will tell you
to jump into the pool.
And yet the pool will remain?
Possibly, says Brother.

And I, unjumped, will remain?

I believe you will remain, says Brother.

Then obviously you must go to Gloria.

Without a doubt, says Brother.

Minutes go by.

Brother is still.

Brother?

One whole day goes by.

Evening surrounds us.

Morning comes.

Although I am in love with Gloria, resumes Brother, I have not the heart to go to Gloria until you jump into the pool.

Could Gloria come to you?

Her magnificence makes this impossible, says Brother.

I just had a thought.

What's to think about? asks Brother.

The pool.

What else? asks Brother.

Jumping into it.

What else? asks Brother.

The Balkans.

Their winters are heavy, says Brother.

Beautifully heavy.
Like the bones of one thousand grandmothers.
Heavier, says Brother.

Has Gloria ever traveled to The Balkans?
Many times, says Brother.
This is why I love her, says Brother.
Whereas Gloria's ventures are fraught with peril, mine are fraught with no peril, says Brother.
This makes Gloria better than me, says Brother.
And me.
And you, says Brother.

Jump into the pool, says Brother.
It appears Grandmother has built a ship.
Normally, says Brother, shipbuilding takes place in a specialized facility called a shipyard.
In this case, says Brother, Grandmother has used the pool.
Jump into the pool, says Brother. Afterwards you can climb aboard.
The ship holds upwards of thirty men.
Grandmother is perched on the bow.

Very perched, says Brother.

Very, very perched.

I have never seen Grandmother so perched.

When she looks up, says Brother, we'll all be dead.

Even Gloria?

Especially Gloria, says Brother.

Such is the suddenness of living, says Brother.

And loving?

Same thing, says Brother.

Such is the suddenness of loving, says Brother.

Jump into the pool, says Brother.

THE ROSTER

I should never have accepted the gig at Shadow College. I was young, though. Foolish. When I received the offer I was teaching literature and poetry as an adjunct at a large university. I was underpaid, the permanent faculty despised me, and the English Department secretary had started refusing me letterhead. My students had disappeared, as had the chair in my office. My evaluations were blank at best. Occasionally an associate professor would give me the finger in the mailroom. Even the director of creative writing who loved everybody could not love me.

So I took the gig.

Shadow was a small, private college. I was told there was a forest nearby, and a good bookstore in town. My teaching load would be light. My salary would quadruple. I'd be on the tenure track and could look forward to sabbaticals and health benefits (even dental). I was thrilled, as I'd had a terrible toothache for years. The students were described as "non-traditional," which I took as older. Older is good, I thought. The older the better.

I was given only one class to teach the first semester so that I had enough time, as the dean put it, "to find my bearings." He brushed some dust off his bowtie and touched me on the arm. "We don't," he insisted, "want your creative work to wither away due to the demands of the coffin." "Don't you mean," I asked, "the classroom?" "Yes," he said. "That's what I said," he said. "The demands of the classroom." He blushed. "God forbid," he said, "we should be the fly in your ointment." He pointed me in the direction of my classroom and gave me a little push. "Consider us the ointment in your ointment," he said. "As a matter of fact," he continued, "consider our college a flyswatter of sorts. A surplus of ointment." Never for a moment did it seem this dean believed he had taken the idiom too far. Never in my life did I respect a man more.

I felt idealistic for the first time in years. And with this feeling I entered the classroom. The students were already seated. Their heads already were bent over their notebooks. This would be, I thought, a slice of very terrific cake. Based on my experience, the fact they even were present was astonishing. I introduced myself and handed out the syllabus. Because this was an advanced creative writing workshop, I emphasized the success of the class depended on the students. I was merely there, I promised, as a guide who would abandon them at the most beautiful and terrifying point of their journey. I asked them to go around the room and introduce themselves.

Emily was first. She held her notebook over her face. Only her eyes showed. She was barely audible. I caught something about god and punctuation. She spoke as if there were a dash permanently lodged in her throat. I was relieved when the notebook slipped from her tiny, white

hands and with great clarity and longing she began to
speak of a master who I took for her muse. This is good, I
thought. This one's got passion. Bruno was next. In lieu of
introducing himself he stood up, walked over to the light
switch, and began flicking on and off the lights. "Bruno," I
said, "please sit down." He sat down. He was very frail. He
spoke in Polish. He slowly peeled a hard-boiled egg, and
as he peeled I knew somewhere deep in my heart he wrote
of attics, and fathers, and birds. Walter was next. He was
round and sad. He put his arm around Bruno and gener-
ously volunteered to be his translator. It would be a burden, he admitted, but a necessary task. Unfortunately, he
could not stay. He'd be back next week, he promised. He
wrung his hands. He apologized. He had lost a briefcase
that contained his writing. He was nervous. He hoped it
would be returned to him. "Eternally," he added. He loped
out the door, mumbling something about a collector and
angels. Samuel could not go on. "You must go on," I said.
"We are going around the room." Samuel agreed he must
go on. But he could not go on. Gertrude was next. There
was something about her hair that suggested she dwelled
in a continuous present. She spoke in imperatives, and as

she spoke she drew tiny boxes in her notebook. Although nothing like the others, she seemed to belong to them inexplicably. And finally came Franz. He confided to us he'd awoken that morning to find himself sitting in the classroom. He apparently had no idea how he'd gotten there. He was clearly shaken. He asked that we not bring apples to class. He was terrified of apples.

To say these students seemed familiar would be a vast understatement. The smell of old books drifted off them and combined to make what I can only describe as a tiny maelstrom in the middle of the classroom. They seemed *underlined*. If a face could be the face of a person stared at too long, this is how their faces appeared.

I loved them. I loved them fiercely. The fact we met only once a week quickly became unbearable. I could not get them out of my head. In class they barely noticed me. "Walter," Emily would say, "tell Bruno to capitalize the horse." "Which one?" asked Walter. "The one that becomes very small like a wooden toy." "And while you're at it," bellowed Gertrude, "tell Bruno to stop drawing pictures of my feet." "Drop it," warned Walter. I loved how they were as tender as they were harsh with one another. Many times I tried to speak, but my mouth filled up with stones. They carried on as if I wasn't there. "What," I once heard Franz whisper to Emily, "is Samuel waiting for?" Samuel often stared out the window as if someone was coming soon to pick him up. "Hey Franz," said Samuel, "I heard you." They wrestled for a few minutes and then broke into the strangest laughter I've ever had the pleasure of hearing. "Emily," said Gertrude ignoring the boys, "maybe you should consider turning these poems into prose poems." "In your dreams," said Emily.

I would see them moving down the halls of the English Department in deep discussion and I'd say, "Hi guys," but they never saw me. Never heard me. I became feverish with longing. I stopped sleeping, stopped eating, stopped bathing. Sometimes in class I would lie down in the middle of the floor and hope they would pile on top of me. Smother me. I wanted to be the coats they wore. I wanted to be the scarves around their necks.

I began following them home. One by one. Once I even pressed my lips on Samuel's window, and left behind a slightly shaken, mushy lipstick mark. I carved my name into a tree in Gertrude's yard. I rummaged through Emily's trash. I left a box of macaroons on Bruno's porch with a note that read *forever yours.* I collected train schedules for Franz and stuffed them in his mailbox. And because Walter never did find his briefcase, I bought him a dozen of them—expensive leather briefcases that cost me three months of my salary. I left them on his doorstep, knocked, and ran away.

Like most stories of obsession this one doesn't end with scandal or murder or permanent ruin. One day, in the middle of the semester, I just packed up my bags and took the bus to my mother's. I was at the end of my rope, and it was either the void or I'd have to shinny back up. Retrace my steps. Get out of there quick. Go back to the beginning. No one, to my knowledge, ever realized I was gone. What mark could my absence possibly make? I was obsolete from the very beginning. Except for that one beautiful moment when I asked Bruno to please sit down and he sat down, did those students ever hear one word that came out of my mouth? "And that time," my mother reminds me, "when you told Samuel he must go on but he could not go on." She says this to console me. "Yes," I say. "That was fantastic."

After my short stay at Shadow College I quit teaching. I work in a post office now. Tomorrow they issue the Eclipse Stamp. I hear pressing on it reveals the image of the full moon. Once it cools, it will return to a white halo around a black disk.

THE TAXMEN

When the taxmen come for Father's heart, Father is on the phone. I hear him say, "they're here." I hear him say, "keep the bones." And then there is a long pause and then he says, "in a bucket, a bucket." And then he says something about the moon, or ruin, or home. Lately, Father's skin has seemed the color of fog.

Already his suits have been confiscated. His beautiful long beard shaved. Even the crows have been taken, one by one. There are so many debts. For failure to satisfy, they have already seized Mother. She writes to us from where they keep her, but her letters are gaunt and drowsy. When she signs her name it is like her name is drifting away. The taxmen are knocking. They are shouting for Father. "Wald-baums, open up!"

Father looks at me and I nod, and by nodding I encourage him to be himself.

Father takes a deep breath. Father looks down. In a small voice he asks, "Did I not hold each of you to my bosom? Did I not bring you the bouquets of lamb's ear you specifi-cally requested? Did I not kiss you in the dark one thou-sand times?"

"Open up, Waldbaums!"

And then even softer. "Did I not draw each of you in char-coal forever?"

"Open up, Waldbaums!"

And then even softer. "Did I not carry your babies from the village as the village burned?"

"Open up, Waldbaums!"

I am beginning to wonder how it is possible for Father to owe this much.

"Open up, Waldbaums!"

It's useless. Father tells me to open up. He stands behind me. Since morning, Father has been getting smaller. Yesterday he towered above me. Now he comes up to my knees.

There are rows and rows of men in short-sleeved button-downs as far as I can see. They spill into the neighbors' yards. Each waves a small red flag. They sit cross-legged. They are smiling.

"Go away," I shout. But Kraus, their leader, who is on horseback, looks past me. "We have come for your father's beautiful heart," says Kraus. He is drinking 2% milk straight out of the container. "Step aside," he says. "This feels like a dream," says Father. "But this is no dream," says

Kraus. "This is as real as your life will ever get." There is milk gathering at the corners of Kraus's lips.

I begin to wonder what Kraus would look like frozen and thawed. His head is so small and pointy, like a steeple. In this way he seems vulnerable to lightning.

"Governmentally," says Kraus, "we have permission this year to go in deeper than usual. Please hand over your heart of the matter, your matter of the heart, your matted heart, your heart psalm, your heart palm, hand over your palm, close it, close it up, Waldbaums, hand over your fist, your fist the size of your heart, your fistfight, your burst heart, your heart thirst, don't thrust it, Waldbaums, hand it over tenderly, it is your most tenderest thingamajig, wrap your heart in a handkerchief with black hearts all over it, hand over your blackest, blacked out heart, your happily ever after heart, your hollow heart, hand over chambers one through three, four you can keep, four you can use for your personable needs, your perishable needs, also the valves, Waldbaums, hand them over, also the superior vena cava, also the super cave, and the veins, and the reigns, your rainy heart, your arterial art, your throaty heart of a heart, hand over your heart you old heartthrob, oh you Waldbaumy Waldbaums, balmy Waldbaums, silly Waldbaums, give us your steamy, smoky hearty-heart-heart before we blow your house down."

The taxmen giggle. They wander into Father's house. Unlike wolves, they seem sleepy and friendly.

Kraus dismounts. I realize his legs are two sticks. Like in a drawing. He follows us around the house, stiffly.

"I do not wish to fight this *guerre* any longer," says Father. "Just bring their leader, Kraus, my heart." By now Father is so small I carry him around in my hand. All over the house, the taxmen scurry happily. Kraus stays close to father and me. One stick in front of the other. I open the oven where Father keeps his heart. In one hand I hold Father, and in the other I bring his heart gently to my nose. It smells like ivory soap. It is heavier than I remember. I lean Father against it so he can breathe his heart in for the last time.

I look over at Kraus. He is holding a balloon. His mouth is the letter O. I close my eyes and open them. Now Kraus is a drawing of a little boy taped to the wall. Father's heart is the red sun above Kraus's head.

Now the taxmen are not men but drawings of little boys taped to the wall. Their soft, sweet eyes. Their red lips. Running wild through fields of flowers. Boys and flowers, boys and flowers, boys and flowers. And look, there's Father too. As a little boy. All paid up. Owing nothing. He is running and laughing. "Come out," I say. "Come out. Come out wherever you are." "But we cannot come out," laughs Father, "we are playing." Father tries to hide but I see him everywhere. I reach in and pluck him out. A small dry boy the size of a cricket. I punch a hole through Father and fasten him around my neck with a thick, blue yarn. I press Father to my throat. My oval gem. My dark inheritance. And it's just like he promised. That it would all, one day, belong to me.

TWO JOKES WALK INTO A BAR

Two jokes walk into a bar. The bartender says he'll be back in three shakes of a lamb's tail and disappears in broad daylight out the front door. The jokes hold hands and wait for the bartender to return. A third joke walks in. He clears his throat, and then, off the top of his head, he begins: "A little Madness in the Spring / Is wholesome even for the King, / But God be with the Clown — / Who ponders this tremendous scene —." "Emily Dickinson," says the first joke. "Nicely done." The third joke is genuinely impressed. It is rare a joke so quickly gets it. All three jokes hold hands and wait for the bartender to return. The second joke's father is dying, but he doesn't want to talk about it. Instead he thinks about the bartender who will be back once the lamb's tail shakes three times. Why is it "shake" of a lamb's tail, and not "wag"? "Wag" suggests the lamb is happy and free, while "shake" sounds like "shank," which brings to the table the lamb's dumb truth: It will eventually be eaten. The jokes hold hands and wait for the bartender to return. The bartender's name is Bob. Bob Oranges. He's a friendly if slightly boring guy who will never return, and somewhere deep inside, the jokes know this already. From far off there is the faintest sound of children playing. It is noon and the jokes are in a bar. "If we were the Fates," poses the second joke, "which one of us do you think would hold the scissors?" Jokes one and three laugh nervously because this is clearly a rhetorical question. There is no way a joke would parade as a Fate. Most jokes would sooner drown themselves. The jokes warn the second joke not to even joke about this. But the second joke is angry. His father is dying. The first joke exchanges a worried look with the third. "Did I tell you about the dream I had last night?" The first joke is trying to lighten the mood. "Franz Kafka was walking up and down this beach. It looked a lot like the one I used to go to as a kid. You know, where I'd build sandcastles and stuff." He pauses, smirks. "So in this dream I walk toward Kafka, and as I approach I realize he's singing 'Try a Little Tenderness.' Like full blast. Like really belting it out." Just as the jokes are about to laugh, a bartender walks into the bar. It is not Bob Oranges. It is a different bartender. "What did I miss?" asks the bartender. The first joke tells him his dream. The bartender laughs and says, "Them young girls they *do* get wearied . . . wearing that *ooooold* shabby dress." The bartender drags out "old" like he's pulling off a sock that won't let go. At "dress," he gets a faraway look as if he has a girl in mind. The door opens. Day floods in. A rabbi and a priest walk into the bar. It seems, distantly, as if something like this has happened before. To the jokes, these men look familiar. The first and third joke offer the men their seats. It is the only respectful thing to do. The priest and the rabbi sit on either side of the second joke, who doesn't seem to notice them. The priest, the joke, and the rabbi hold hands and wait for the bartender to ask them what they're having. But now this bartender is else-where, most likely still thinking about a girl he once knew and possibly loved. The priest and the rabbi want to say something about wonder and tenderness and love and life and death, but they can't think of anything. Their minds have gone blank. The second joke frees his hands from the soft grip of the men to light a cigarette, and as he does his cell phone rings. It rings, and rings, and rings. But the joke's not going to get it. Not this one. Not now. No siree, Bob . . . Oranges, thinks the second joke. And at this he chuckles, because he knows it'll be the last funny thing for a long, long time.

THE MAID, THE MOTHER,
THE SNAIL & I

The maid is not herself. She hands me a can of Easy Off and walks away. The kitchen is not clean. The bathroom is not clean. The beds are unmade. Something is bothering the maid. Her long white arms seem longer than usual.

It's barely eight and already she has dropped the mop, causing a serious bang and scaring me half to death. Now she is hiding in the bathroom eating an entire can of sardines. I hear her pull back the tin lid to get to the last one. It sends a shiver through the house. Something is bothering the maid. The refrigerator's hum because of her is off. All the vegetables are dead. The milk, like a ghost, is turning. By noon she will ask me (as she now asks me everyday) if I love her. Why does the maid ask me this? Isn't it obvious? And then half past the same hour she will ask me what moon I am. Waxing or waning? How do I know what moon? She has lost her sense of precision. Her technique is off. If she ever had a plot her plot is long gone. She has forgotten to bring Mother Mother, who is dying in the livingroom, her pills. She has abandoned a pink sponge on the stovetop. The maid is not herself. It has been a lousy winter. The maid has begun to smell a lot like ash. Frankly, she has begun to smell like an en-tire house burnt to the ground. She has neglected Bye Bye Françoise, the family parakeet, whose cage is in shambles. And now Bye Bye Françoise is not herself, though Bye Bye Françoise is more herself than the maid is herself given the maid is less and less herself as each hour passes. She has replaced the grocery list with #1 a prelude to nothing #2 a war poem, leaving me with no idea of what we need. Bread? Eggs? Sparkling water? It's anybody's guess. Who does the maid think she is? Herself or not herself?

The maid and I once were best friends. I called her Lydia, and she called me Lydia though our names were nowhere near Lydia. We knew how to be everything: rubber, dirt, glass, wire. We even knew how to be children. We even knew how to be happy. Now the maid stands at the kitchen sink, still as stone. And I stand beside her waiting for the dirty, dirty dishes to be washed and dried. "Lydia, are you there? Lydia?" No answer.

I cannot stop thinking about the maid. Mother Mother, who is dying in the livingroom, urges me to rest. "But the maid is not herself." "Of course the maid is not herself," says Mother Mother. "How could the maid possibly be herself?" I lie beside Mother Mother's quietly dying soft, brown body, and fall asleep and dream I am walking up and down the aisles of a supermarket. In my cart is an old orange. It costs seven thousand dollars, and when I open my purse all I have is an ocean. "We do not accept," says the cashier who is really the maid who is not herself, "an ocean." The waves crash, which embarrasses me.

I wake up against an area of Mother Mother that has been designed to rot. No doctor can explain why.

It is possible the maid is a Jew, which could explain why the maid is not herself, though I have never asked her whether or not she is a Jew. Mother Mother is a Jew and I am a Jew and Father Father (who is missing) is a Jew. I read somewhere that some Jews escaped Poland by hiding in coffins. We are more or less ourselves, given our history, but the maid (Jew or not a Jew) seems more not herself than necessary. Around her head, she has begun wearing a silk scarf printed all over with tiny hatchets. Hatchets she will never bury.

The maid and I go outside. I say something and she disagrees. Snowflakes begin falling on her head, but not on mine. The maid points to a swimming pool in the far distance. "You see that swimming pool?" "Barely," I say. "As a child, I swam in that swimming pool. I didn't drown once." The maid and I hold hands and walk eleven blocks before we run into Sweetie Pie, my maid before my maid who is not herself. Sweetie Pie is pink and fat. She shakes my maid hard until a small snail falls out. Sweetie Pie picks up the snail, cleans its shell carefully on her flowery dress, and hands it to me. "Did you know," says Sweetie Pie, "that snail shells and the inner ear follow the same spiral?" "No," I say. "That is how we know the snails are listening." "Oh, I say." I look at Sweetie Pie. I miss her so much, but not as much as I miss the maid who is not herself. I give the maid back her snail. She pops it into her mouth and sucks on it like it's hard candy. "I am sorry," I say to Sweetie Pie. "I know so little about snails, and now the maid who is not herself and I need to go home." Sweetie Pie looks at the maid hard. "How is she with floors?" she asks. "Left to right or right to left?" "Nowhere," I answer.

In the morning, I look in the mirror until my reflection thins enough for me to see Mother Mother staring back at me and then it thins again and there's the maid.

I scrub the house. I check on Bye Bye Françoise. I clean her cage. I wipe her perch. Bye Bye Françoise is not herself. Her eyes are black and still. I gently pet her small blue feathery head, but she turns her head away. I dust the sills. I beat the rugs. I polish the banisters. I wash and dry the stacks and stacks of dirty dishes. I change Mother Mother's sheets. I brush her hair. I apply rose-scented gloss to her lips. I empty her darkening bags of fluid. I give her the pills.

My work doesn't matter. There is always dirt. There are always things where they should never be. The minute I look away, what wasn't a mess will become a mess and the mess will be a holy one.

"Are you fed?" asks Mother Mother. "No," I say, "I'm fine." "There are wonder cakes," says Mother Mother. She touches her lips with her thumb. "I left them for you somewhere. Long ago and far away." I take Mother Mother's hand. "Go eat them," she says. "I will," I say. "Go eat them forever."

I leave Mother Mother to go looking for wonder cakes. I find a trail of wrappers leading me straight to the maid who is hunched in the pantry. "Lydia?" Lydia doesn't turn her head. "Remember when you wiped all my countertops until they glistened? Remember when you swept up all the dust? Remember the broom?" She slowly turns, then smiles at me for the first time in months. White and yellow wonder cake crumbs fall gently, like snow, from her mouth.

I bring Mother Mother a glass of water with a pink straw. She takes a sip, but the water doesn't reach her lips. It rises slowly, stops, gives up, and falls. "This is what the end looks like," says Mother Mother. "How about that?" "How about what?" I ask, though I know. "That," says Mother Mother. For a second she drifts off, but the bony sunshine snaps her awake. "Your skull once grew inside me," says Mother Mother. "I know," I say. "I know you know," says Mother Mother. "And now there are these falling children. Make it stop." I do something with my hands, like untying a pretend knot. "Thank you," says Mother Mother. "They have stopped," says Mother Mother. "Except for one. One is still falling, but she is quiet and I don't mind." She takes my hand. "She looks," says Mother Mother squinting up at the air, "just like you."

It is impossible to describe how much I miss the maid. I write her a note.

Dear Lydia,

It is so obvious you got into my collection. My Apple Snail, my Great Pond Snail, and my Trumpet Snail are missing. I still have my Red Spotted Snail, the Crown Snail, and all my Mystery Snails (four). I didn't want to say anything to Sweetie Pie about my vast knowledge of snails. I didn't want to give it away. I was protecting you, Lydia, like you once protected me. I want to shake you like Sweetie Pie shook you until all the snails fall out. I want to jump into the swimming pool you never drowned in as a child. I want you to clean my whole entire house again. It is so dank.

Forever Yours,
Lydia

I fold the note seven times. I find the maid curled up on the disheveled bath rug. She is sound asleep. From her beauty, my heart just mildews. I don't think she will ever clean my house again. I open her gigantic white hand, then close it around my letter.

I follow a long, thin blur of dirt back to Mother Mother. "You should've drawn a line," says Mother Mother, "between you and the maid." "I did," I say, "but it was shaped like an arrow pointing in the direction of my heart." There is so much grime in the air it coats my skin and makes it sticky. "Did you know," says Mother Mother, "that an assembly of snails is called a rout?" Mother Mother's legs seem to be completely disappearing beneath the crumpled sheets. "What's a rout?" I ask. "A disorderly retreat of defeated troops," says Mother Mother. "That makes sense," I say.

One week later, I look out the dirty window and see the maid standing in the yard. As if waiting for a trumpet to sound, her body has turned skyward. I leave her alone. I go to Bye Bye Françoise's cage. Bye Bye Françoise is not there. In her place is a Milk Snail. I've always wanted a Milk Snail. I peel it off Bye Bye Françoise's perch. It waves its tentacles, sleepily. I bring it into the living-room, where Mother Mother is no longer dying. I put the Milk Snail in her bed, and climb in beside it. The bed sheets are so sour. I call for the rest of my collection to join us. The whole rout. They will come. I am certain of it. I just need to be patient. They are snails. And it will, as everything does, take forever.

ARE YOU MY MOTHER?

Francine Prose, who is my mother, calls to inform me there has been an error, and now she is fairly certain she is not my mother, but someone else's mother. She speaks for a long time, at first nervously, then gradually with great eloquence. After a few hours, she begins to break up. The only thing I can make out is something about "Mary's gorgeous hair." I don't know this Mary, although I wish I did. I pick at my nail polish, "Lucky Lucky Lavender." "Mom," I say. "No," she says. "Call me Fran," she says. And hangs up.

I call my cleaning lady, Hillary Clinton. She doesn't seem to know who I am, though she cleaned my kitchen no more than three days ago. The stove is still glistening. "Are you my mother?" I ask. Silence. I ask again. "Hillary Clinton?" "Yes," she says. "Are you my mother?" More silence. I stare out the window, sunk by Hillary Clinton's remoteness. I decide I will clean my own house from now on. After what feels like days, Hillary Clinton asks me what I'm afraid of. Her attention excites me. I answer swiftly. "Mice, old watering cans, political realities, vibrant colors, hooks, Thursday, wounded things, Shep, sacred music . . ." "Who's Shep?" asks Hillary Clinton. "My grandfather," I say. Silence. Then a heavier silence. I look around my living room. All my upholstery is frayed. "Hillary Clinton?" "Yes?" "All my upholstery is frayed." Silence. I wish I'd never called. It's so obvious Hillary Clinton isn't my mother. She doesn't care about me or my upholstery or my deepest fears at all. If she ever came into my room to tuck me in and kiss me goodnight, I would turn my face away.

I send a letter to Jorie Graham because if Francine Prose is not my mother and Hillary Clinton, my cleaning lady, is not my mother, there is a good chance Jorie Graham is my mother. The letter is very beautiful and describes what happened with Francine Prose and Hillary Clinton and my upholstery and all my hopes and dreams.

Two weeks later I get a letter back. Jorie Graham writes, "Sounds like a case of overwatering. Same thing happens with my plants. Why is everything so goddammed difficult?" At the very bottom in very small writing she writes, "How can I be your mother when I am Jorie Graham. I am not your mother. Have you tried Diana Ross?"

I have, in fact, tried Diana Ross.

If Francine Prose is not my mother, and Hillary Clinton is not my mother, and Jorie Graham is not my mother, and Diana Ross is not my mother, maybe John Berryman is my mother. I go to John Berryman's house and knock on his door. He is dead, but he opens anyway. He is wearing a salmon-colored sweater. "Are you my mother?" I ask. "I am not your mother," says John Berryman. He opens the door wider. "But I could become your mother." Shep, my grandfather, is there. He is wearing an identical salm-on-colored sweater. I step inside. It smells like waffles and liver. "Touch my sweater!" yells Shep. I do not want to touch his sweater. "Touch it!" he roars. I reach my hand out, close my eyes, and touch it. It's incredibly soft. "Like god himself!" he thunders. "Touch John Berry-man's sweater!" John Berryman blushes and moves very close to me. I quickly touch John Berryman's sweater. It's as soft as Shep's sweater, maybe even softer. "You know who gave us these sweaters?" "Who?" I ask. "Your mother," says Shep. "Francine Prose?" I ask. "Francine Prose is not your mother," says Shep. "Then who?" I ask. "Your mother!" yells Shep. I look over at John Berryman. "John Berryman?" I ask. Shep laughs. "John Berryman is not your mother." "But I can become your mother," adds John Berryman. Shep tells me to hold on a minute, disappears into another room, and comes back with a third salmon-colored sweater. "Your mother left this for you," says Shep. "Put it on." I put it on. It is beautiful. It is so beautiful John Berryman begins to cry. I put my arms around him and we are like one enormous salmon-colored sweater. "Don't cry," I say. "There, there," I say.

"What?" asks John Berryman. "There, there," I say again. He sniffs and looks at me quizzically. "It's an expression," I say. "It means it'll be okay." "But it won't be okay," says John Berryman. "It will only get worse." "A lot worse," adds Shep. "How much?" I ask. "A ton," says Shep. "A ton worse," adds John Berryman. "Does my mother know?" I ask. "Of course your mother knows," says Shep. "Will she make it better?" I ask. "She will not make it better," says Shep. "Will she at least try?" I ask. "She will not," says Shep. "Can John Berryman make it better?" I am desperate. "He cannot make it better," says Shep. "He is only your pretend mother." "Why won't my mother make it better?" I ask. Shep looks at John Berryman. John Berryman looks at Shep. "Is the salmon-colored sweater not enough for you?" asks Shep. He looks more disappointed than angry. It is a very beautiful sweater. Soft and warm, and probably very expensive. "Because if it is not enough," says Shep, "give it back." I am feeling brave, and sad, and defiant. I take off the salmon-colored sweater and give it back to Shep. John Berryman begins to cry again. He is not a good mother. I put my arms around him. Without the salmon-colored sweater, I feel very small. Also, I am cold. I shiver. I climb under John Berryman's salmon-colored sweater where it is warm. He is sobbing now, heavily. It is like I am in an ocean and the waves are crashing. I close my eyes.

THE STEPMOTHER

"You smell like Florida. We hate you." The Stepmother knows from the crushed handwriting this note is from The Stepchildren. At the bottom of the note is a drawing of a mouse. The Stepmother wants to know what does the mouse mean. The mouse seems lonely and afraid. Its eyes are too big. The Stepmother peels a hard-boiled egg, eats it very quietly, and thinks about the mouse, and Florida, and smelling like Florida. No one wants to smell like Florida. If The Stepmother had any guts she would go to the yard this instant and paint all the trees white, but The Stepmother has no guts. If The Stepmother had any guts her husband who is the father of The Stepchildren who believe she smells like Florida would come home and see the trees and say what in god's name have you done? Do you think we're living in a goddamn fairy tale here? The Stepmother would stand there with her large bucket of paint, and her guts, and tell her husband the trees are now white because she is not a real Mother, she will never be a real Mother, and also she is thinking of running away with the mouse. She would sob and say something strange and dramatic like how she feels as though she's three plagues short of an exodus even though she doesn't really have any plagues except for smelling like Florida. But none of this will happen because The Stepmother has no guts, and this is America not a fairy tale. This is a state in America that is not Florida even though The Stepmother is reeking of it. The Stepmother wants to know what does the mouse mean. It is a beautiful mouse. The Stepmother has no guts but she does have some scissors which she uses to cut the mouse out. No one wants to be lonely, and afraid, and live in a note about smelling like Florida. Once The Stepmother cuts the mouse out the mouse shivers. It is a very sad shiver. Sadder than all The Stepmother's sadnesses, and somehow this comforts her. The Stepmother isn't certain whether the shiver is from coldness or relief, but she cuts off a strand of her hair and wraps it around the mouse's shoulders anyway. The mouse falls asleep in the palm of The Stepmother's hand, and dreams of guts, and white trees, and the kindness of The Stepmother. The mouse is what the mouse means. It's The Stepchildren who mean something else. It's The Stepchildren who mean something far, far away, like a Mother. When The Stepchildren come home The Stepmother will hug and kiss them and wipe their dirty little hands until their hearts break in two.

THE STICK FIGURE FAMILY

"Something, something is not right," says Mrs. Stick. One of her arms disappears off the page. She uses her other to hold her Stick Babies. Mr. Stick wears a hat. "Honey, I'm home." He enters stiffly. "Something, something is not right," says Mrs. Stick. Mr. Stick takes the babies who are crying sticks and feeds them sticks. Original dread. The Stick Babies are flowering pink. The afternoon is thinning. It is a struggle to be a line. When I go over there, they touch my sweater. They touch my hair. Outside the clouds hang loose like nobody's skin. This family is not mine, though they stare at me like they once were. Mrs. Stick presses her cold, weathered mouth against my cheek and whispers something that sounds like "love, love," though

I can't be sure. For too long she stays against me. Evening comes. Mr. Stick covers the Stick Babies with sticks and prays they sleep and never dream of rocks. "What have I done?" he asks. "Who are these people we once never were?" Mrs. Stick calls out for Mr. Stick. He thickens, frowns, and goes to her. I watch the Stick Babies sleep. Their legs and arms, crossed and thin, make a shadow of cobwebs. I pick the tiny pink flowers off their limbs. They hardly breathe. There are so many flowers. Out of them, I will make a bouquet I will hold to my chest when I walk down the aisle and marry you.

FATHER

"The larger of two carts for moving things," read the message, "is missing from room 255. If you have it please return asap. It is needed." Had the message never appeared in our inboxes, we would've gone on believing Father. But the message appeared, as did Father with the cart.

We wished we had no inboxes. We were mad.

Mad at Father?

Yes, we were mad at Father. But we were mad mostly at ourselves. And at Mary Helen for sending the message. And we were mad at our inboxes.

We were mad as beets.

The conundrum as we saw it was that Father loved us. The larger of two carts for moving things did not love us, nor did Mary Helen, nor did our inboxes. It was in our best interest to take Father's side, to believe there was a flood of carts, a deluge of carts, and the cart now being pulled around our living room like some heartbroken farm animal was not the same cart that had mysteriously gone missing. "But all the evidence," piped up Mendel, "points to Father's malfeasance." Mendel was the smallest of us, and the most committed to truth. I sniffed Mendel's head. He smelled like cucumbers.

It was the last thing we wanted to do, but on Mendel's behest we tromped to our inboxes to further examine the message.

A significant amount of moss had grown over Annette's inbox, which concerned us, but today was not about Annette or her inbox. Today was about Father.

Over Father we were agog. We were gaga. If he told us to hold our horses, with all our might we'd hold our horses even until they all stopped breathing. If he urged us to flee, we'd flee. We glowed like a mob that came night after night only for him. And now just a mouse click away from possible ruin, our child-sized hearts were disheveled with worry.

"This is not the same cart," Father assured us. "This is a different cart."

Which is not to say we hadn't worried before. We had. But the jig that had stayed down for years was now ascending like a tired balloon. "Why," asked Annette, "does there even need to be a jig?" She was pulling on her skirt, as if pulling on her skirt would pull the jig down. She asked this, but she knew. There always has to be a little bit of jig so as to keep our brains from softening. Even so, the very last thing we ever wanted to say to Father was "gotcha!"

The stories Father made up, in the beginning, barely

grazed us. He would tell us about all the years he spent with Mother battening down the hatches when we knew very well there was no mother or hatch for miles. We knew if given the chance Father would have no idea how to batten anything. But we listened, and we forgave.

This was before we had inboxes.

The old ladies would be showing up soon to help us, but in the meantime it was up to us, Father's son and daughters, his "henchmen" as he called us in the summer, his "poppets" as he called us in the winter, to get to the bottom of Father. "The larger," read Mendel, "of two carts . . ." We looked from our inboxes to Father. We looked from Father to the cart. The cart was large. Some might even say *obese*. But how could we be certain the missing cart was not more obese? Father was curled up on top of it like a house cat. He had one gray eye open. We wished the old ladies would hurry up.

We were still huddled over our inboxes when we caught Father sneaking up on us. "Hi," he said. "Hi," said Annette, a little too loudly. "Did you know I was the *sine qua non* of the avant-garde?" asked Father. We shook our heads. "The President called me. Soldiers are shooting at me." "Right now?" asked Mendel, steadily. "Earlier," said Father. The cart looked incredibly sad.

Father wandered out of earshot.

"There is something wrong with it," I whispered to Mendel. "Who?" asked Mendel. "Father?" Well, yes, Father. Often Father. But what I meant was the cart. It looked like it might be sick. There were flies.

The situation was delicate. What we couldn't allow was Father's enthusiasm over us to diminish. "I would absolutely die," said Annette, picking at the moss.

Neither Mendel, nor I, nor Annette, nor Father wanted Annette to die. "If we broke the lines," Mendel suggested, "maybe we could free Father from our suspicions." This was a very good idea.

The larger of two
carts
for moving things is missing

from room 255
if you have it

please return

asap.

It is needed.

We were pleased. That the message was now a poem made it no less a beast, but this beast might one day grow to love us. "All it needs is a title," said Annette. "'Where Is the Cart?'" suggested Mendel. "Or 'The Cart Is Missing.' Or 'What Is Wrong with Father?' Or, simply, 'The Cart.'" I liked the last best. Father said if it was his poem he'd call it "L'état, C'est Moi," which meant, "I Am the Cart." But we knew very well it did not mean that.

The old ladies arrived at approximately five o'clock, which was too late to change the course of our childhoods. We were, as Annette put it, "poem or no poem: fucked." "Annette!" we cried. "That is such a curse!" There were so many times Mendel, Annette, and I wanted to just look out the window of a moving car and regard the terrain, but with the old ladies showing up as late as they did, and the cold fact of our inboxes, and our motherlessness, and the cart possibly dying in our living room, and god knows what always wrong with Father, we knew that wish was a long way off. We were not the kind of children who would ever one day be passengers. We showed the old ladies the poem. "C'est magnifique," said the old ladies, kissing the tips of their fingers.

By dinner Father was still going at it. "Among the Lebanese poets," said Father, "I'm considered a real muckamuck. Among the French, I'm practically Pulitzer." Annette was cutting a piece of steak so hard her knife slipped on the plate and flew across the room, landing on the cart. From where I was sitting it looked like the knife had cut the cart. It looked like there was a little blood.

At first, we thought Mendel got up from the table to nurse the wounded cart, but his brow was furrowed in another direction. Our appetites were gone. The soup the old ladies had brought us was cold enough to taste ruined. I looked over at Annette. Something very unsunlike shone on her face. It was our inboxes again. Our inboxes were blinking. That was where Mendel was going. To our inboxes.

The recipients were us. The sender, as always, was Mary Helen. Our inboxes held the message, freshly opened, like a bag of fake bread.

"We are children, for christsake," cried Annette. "Why do we even have inboxes, when we barely have money? Even Father has no inbox." This was true. Father's inbox, he claimed, had been taken away. "One day," Father whispered, "a man I'd never seen before just yoinked my inbox out from under me. You're lucky you still have yours." And when Father told us this we felt lucky. Luckier than ever. Now we were not so sure.

Dutifully, Annette and I tromped back to our inboxes and joined Mendel. "The larger of two fathers for moving things," read the message, "is missing from room 255. If you have him please return asap. He is needed." We looked over at Father. He wasn't where we left him. We looked over at the cart. A small pool of blood had settled under its left hind wheel. Outside, it was raining. Had we ever really been children, we definitely were no longer. We were old. Older than Father. Older than the old ladies. Older than the dying cart. Our inboxes were receiving messages we really could no longer accept. Mendel wheeled the cart outside. We knew by morning it would be dead in our yard. From what Father had taught us, we understood there was no way to stop the dying from dying. If this, in fact, was true. There was nothing we could do to save it. We had no way of knowing anything.

I DID NOT EAT THE CHILD

A stepchild, I'm sorry, is a ghost. Mine is called Ugrit.

To her face, her father calls her Ugrit the Holy. Holy, for short. To not her face her father calls her nothing, barely remembers her. "Where did you put Ugrit, Husband?" And Husband says, "Who?" And then he touches his beard and remembers. "I put her outside to dry." And there she is, pacing back and forth beneath a clothesline, parched and gigantic.

I open the screen door. "Ugrit, come in."

Over Ugrit, my heart is a fistfight. She is never my progeny, but when there is the hen for dinner I must buy Ugrit the hen. Husband and I have other, real children for whom I never question buying the hen. Only for Ugrit do I question buying the hen, as I question buying the surrounding vegetables, as I question buying the cold milk and the underpants.

"I do not wish to buy and cook and slice and serve Ugrit the hen." "Who?" asks Husband. "Ugrit! Ugrit!" "But there is leftover hen," says Husband. "There is so much hen. Give Holy some hen." It is true. There is so much hen. But I am exhausted of Ugrit and the hen she needs. "She needs so little hen," whispers Husband. "Just give her some hen. She is my flesh and she is my bone." I do not wish to give Ugrit the hen, but without me she is so henless. It is too much henlessness to bear. And so I give her hen too. This is the problem with hunger. This is the problem with love. There is no end in sight.

Sometimes I think what does it matter. Like all the hens I've ever forgotten for whole entire days, and there have been many, we too will one day shrivel up to nothingness.

Ugrit the Holy. Ugrit of Over There. Ugrit the Ghost. Ugrit of Not Mine.

"How is the hen, Ugrit?" "Gaunt," she replies.

After dinner, she creeps up to me. I cannot tell if she is sleeping or awake. She is hunched, like always. I throw bunches of roses at her, hoping a curtain might come down followed by great applause, hoping to end the scene of Ugrit. But she keeps coming closer. Her mouth is a thin moon of frantic light. I kiss her on the cheek and she coughs up a heart the size of a marble. She spits it into my hand. "Whose heart is this, Ugrit?" It is wet and I am disgusted. She shrugs. She pretends she doesn't know the heart is so obviously her mother's. And then she creeps away.

I do not want this tiny mother heart Ugrit coughs up. I give it to Husband, which I know is a mistake. He tells me he'll bury it before it grows wild. But he never buries it. At night I hear it clicking against his teeth. It moves around his mouth like a hard candy animal, circling for comfort.

This child named Ugrit is not my child. She is another woman's child. Being near Ugrit makes it impossible to be near a beautiful sea.

"How is the hen, Ugrit?" "Gaunt," she replies.

For my birthday Ugrit bakes me a cake. The piece she slices for me is still pinkish and mewing. The rest of the cake is still. I tell Husband I want him to send Ugrit away. "Who?" asks Husband. "Ugrit! Ugrit!" He bounces the other, real children on his knee. They are so healthy and cheerful! "Who?" asks Husband. "Ugrit!" I say, but he cannot hear me over our other, real children.

Sometimes I wonder if Ugrit even knows my name.

"Happy Birthday, Stepmother," says Ugrit. "Thank you, Ugrit." "Are you happy, Stepmother?" I look at Ugrit. I really look at her. She is not resplendent in her heavy corduroy pants. "No, Ugrit, I am not happy." "Because your slice is pinkish and mewing, Stepmother?" "Partially, Ugrit." "What else, Stepmother?" "Because, Ugrit, I do not know what to carry into this unfolding epoch." Ugrit brings her face close to mine. "Shovels and water?" she asks.

In the morning there is a bucket and a small, shiny shovel leaning against my bedroom door.

"Thank you, Ugrit."

I cannot find the rest of Ugrit's story. Believe me, I search. I go out walking. I wait for the air to thin so I can for once see something clearly. But the air rarely thins, and even when it does it's always just Ugrit standing there. Staring. Waiting for something I will never dream up. She does not cry, but sometimes she holds my own crying mother in her arms. My own inconsolable, crying mother.

I cannot remember life without Ugrit.

"Stepmother?" "Yes, Ugrit." "May I have more?" "More what, Ugrit?" "Never mind," says Ugrit. "Please Ugrit, more what?" "Ugrit. More Ugrit." "Take as much Ugrit as you'd like." She goes to the place where Ugrit is kept and she takes more. She knows I disapprove, but she cannot help it. When Ugrit helps herself to more Ugrit there is a humming in the house that lasts for days. One day we will run out of hen, but we will never run out of Ugrit. Of Ugrit there is galore.

I ask Husband again to send Ugrit away. "How can I choose," asks Husband, "between Heaven and Sorry?" And I know he's right. It's impossible to choose. She will stay. The other, real children will grow up and kiss me on the forehead and leave. But Ugrit will stay.

"How is the hen, Ugrit?" "Gaunt," she replies.

Click, click, click goes the tiny mother heart.

While Husband and Ugrit and the other, real children sleep, I sneak into Ugrit's room. I pile on all her clothes. I enter the cotton and corduroy and fleece and wool until I can barely move or breathe. I do not know why I do this. I want to tell Ugrit to go on without me, but it is becoming harder and harder.

In the morning, it is Ugrit who finds me. She lifts me up out of the cocoon. "I am so hot, Ugrit, and so thirsty." She brings me the bucket of water. It is the same bucket she left for me to carry into the unfolding epoch. I take a sip. The water tries to climb up out of my mouth. I swallow hard. It is like slaughter. "I cannot drink this water, Ugrit. This water is alive." Ugrit takes the bucket away. I wipe my mouth. I notice a bruise on Ugrit's arm. It too is alive because everything is alive. The bruise on Ugrit's arm is in the shape of a hen. It is walking toward me. A magnificent hen. Far more beautiful than any hen I've ever cooked to perfection. "Where did you get that hen, Ugrit?" It keeps walking toward me. Ugrit needs to turn that hen around. "Turn that hen around, Ugrit." It walks fast. No hen should walk that fast. "Who hurt you, Ugrit? Why is there a hen on your arm?" The hen looks at me hard. If it were up to me, I would cook her and eat her. I would give some of her to Ugrit too, angrily. Torn. Ugrit hands me the small shiny shovel. The hen walks toward me fast. I take the shovel. I hold it up. It is so shiny. Here comes the hen. I can almost see my face.

LET'S DO THIS ONCE MORE, BUT THIS TIME WITH FEELING

Louis C.K., my husband, piles all my seahorses in the middle of our king-sized bed and starts shouting. I see moon-and-stars seahorse, and green seahorse, and the one with no eyes, and pink seahorse, and says-things seahorse, and pregnant seahorse, and I see the sad one, but I don't see black seahorse. "Where is black seahorse, Louis?" This makes Louis C.K., my husband, even angrier. In a fake little girl voice, all sing song, he goes "WheRe is BlAcK SeAhoRSe, LoUIs!?" My husband, Louis C.K., is not being very nice. So I say, "No, not black seahorse Louis, just black seahorse," which makes Louis roar. So I say, "What's the matter Louis? Why so boiled?"

"What does your anger, Louis, have to do with my seahorses?"

We go through this every night.

In the morning everything is fine.

Louis C.K. and I hold hands. We go to the meadow and make love. We do not bring up the seahorses. Louis pulls my head all the way back. He kisses my throat. His lips are rough like rope. I call out, "Sweet, Sweet Nothing." "Who?" asks Louis. He looks around. "Who," he asks, "is Sweet, Sweet Nothing?" "You," I say, though it's impossible to be sure.

I cannot explain it but ever since the seahorses Louis and I have become less and less human. Our ability to speak has gone from stratospheric to cloudy. "Tell me about eternity, Louis." And Louis tells me all about eternity using mostly the wildflowers from the meadow. For hours and hours, with the petals and stems, he builds boats and whole entire cities and nations of people with terrible long flowing hair, but nothing really comes of it. He speaks for a long time, but the words are few and far between and half-finished. Like somewhere in the middle of being words they closed their eyes and fell asleep and dreamed they were seahorses.

When we get home Louis C.K., my husband, piles all my seahorses in the middle of our queen-sized bed and starts shouting. "I thought, Louis, we had a king-sized bed." Our bed now is unquestionably queen, which makes the seahorses look larger than they did the night before. Black seahorse is still missing. Louis doesn't answer or look at me. He just keeps piling and shouting and piling and shouting. I see super seahorse and old seahorse and nowhere seahorse and sorry seahorse and the one the other seahorses call the Saint and the one they call the Fool.

We go through this every night.

In the morning everything is fine.

Louis C.K. and I go to the diner. We sit in our favorite booth. "I love you," says Louis. "I love you more," I say. We hold hands. We are very alive. The waitress takes our order. Louis orders two soft-boiled eggs, coffee, and toast with strawberry jam. I order the same. We do not bring up the seahorses. The waitress's name is Poppy. She is wearing a T-shirt with a blue and red rocket ship. Poppy serves us our breakfast. "Where is the rocket ship going?" asks Louis. Poppy looks at me. I shrug. I have no idea. Poppy looks at Louis. She looks down at the rocket ship. "Isn't it always going to the moon?" asks Poppy. "I guess so," says Louis. There is a little bit of jam on Louis' cheek. Poppy dips a napkin into my water glass and wipes it off. She kisses Louis on the mouth. He kisses her back. They kiss for a long, long time. "Don't be wounded," she whispers. "Don't be wounded more," he whispers back. While they kiss I build a tower out of all the jams and pats of butter and honeys. I collect them from all the booths. The tower is so high I have to stand on the table to keep building. At the very top, I imagine perching hold-me seahorse and never-let-me-go seahorse, but seconds before Louis and Poppy finally stop kissing the whole tower comes toppling down.

"Is that all there is?" asks Louis. We look around. It seems it is. The diner is empty. Jams and butters and honeys are everywhere. Poppy has disappeared into the kitchen. Possibly forever. We look out the window. Out on the street are a few orange and red and green bouncing balls neither Louis nor I have even seen before, but otherwise not much else. Our friend Ferguson runs past us. I knock hard on the glass and call out, "Hey, Ferguson, is that all there is?" But he doesn't hear me. "Go on without us," calls out Louis. But Ferguson has already gone on.

"Look," says Louis. "Something fell out of Ferguson's pocket." Louis and I rush out of the empty diner to see what it is. Two identical black seahorses lie on their sides. Their heads are touching. I am careful not to get too close. There is something wrong with these seahorses. It is possible their heads are attached. It is possible neither one is my black seahorse. It is possible they are not alive.

"So is THAT all there is?" asks Louis. He waves his arms around, messily. He seems angry. I don't know if by THAT he means the seahorses or my feelings about the seahorses or my still missing black seahorse or the flash of Ferguson or the broken tower forever ruined or the orange and red and green bouncing balls which are all still bouncing or life in general or eternity or his undying love for me which might be dying a little on account of the seahorses and on account of kissing Poppy.

When we get home Louis C.K., my husband, piles all our seahorses in the middle of our twin bed and starts shouting. I think back to the two identical black seahorses. What, if anything, belongs to me? I mean, really belongs to me? I look up at Louis. Our bed is shrinking. Every day he destroys me. And every day I destroy him in return. Little tiny bits of destroying. It's barely noticeable. We have a baby somewhere, but it is too small. Louis is piling and shouting and piling and shouting. I see bruise seahorse and growling seahorse and rotten seahorse and close-up seahorse and wooden seahorse and happy seahorse and the empty one, but

I don't see black seahorse. I call Ferguson. He doesn't answer. I leave a message.

We go through this every night. In the morning everything is fine.

"Louis?" "Yes, Seahorse?" Louis calls me Seahorse. "Have we gotten to the sad part yet?" "Yes, Seahorse, we have."

"When do we get to the funny part, Louis?" "Soon," says Louis. "Soon."

Louis C.K. and I go to the misty boneyard. Ferguson is there. He is swaying back and forth, like he's praying. In the middle of the boneyard is a water fountain. I take a sip. Louis takes a sip. He looks around. "Whose bones are these, Seahorse?" I look around. "Probably ours," I say. Louis puts his hand over his mouth and spits. A tooth falls out. A small one. It is hardly essential to Louis' mouth. "Have we gotten to the funny part, Louis?" "No, Seahorse, not yet." He gives me the tooth to hold. I shift it in my palm. It is ice cold.

In the space where Louis' tooth once was is a tiny white seahorse, flashing bright.

We slow dance in the misty boneyard. When Louis isn't looking, I let his tooth fall out of my hand and disappear into a pile of bones.

Ferguson is still swaying. He shakes his fists in the air, opens them, and out flies a shower of black seahorses. I count fifty. Maybe more.

I collect them all. I stuff them into my shirt.

I am hungry. I want more black seahorses because my black seahorse is still missing. Louis C.K., my husband, and I go back to look for the seahorses that yesterday fell out of Ferguson's pocket. It is a long walk from the misty boneyard to the diner. It takes us two full days, but we get there. The seahorses are exactly where we left them. With the tip of his thumb, Louis flips them over and quickly jumps back. The seahorses crack apart. There is writing on each belly.

On one seahorse it says, "I do not belong to you."

On the other seahorse it says, "Neither do I."

Louis begins to laugh. Then I begin to laugh. Then Poppy emerges from the sunshine and she begins to laugh too. We are rolling on the ground laughing. I am laughing so hard my chest hurts. Like I am being shot in the heart over and over and over again by bullets in the shape of all the black seahorses that will never belong to me. I want to ask Louis if this is the funny part, but I am laughing so hard I can barely breathe.

I want to ask Louis if this is the funny part, but when I catch my breath and look up Poppy and Louis are gone. The only one to ask is a police officer whistling in the distance.

In the morning everything is fine.

THE SEVENTH WIFE

When the husband's seventh wife is sad because she was not his first wife or his second or even his third wife the husband brings her fish. He brings her Cod and Sole. He brings her Mackerel, Herring, Eel, Bonnetmouth, Trout, and Bleak. He brings her Barb, Ghost Carp, and Ghoul. The husband does not want his seventh wife to be sad and so he brings her Flounder. He brings her Mullet, Snook, Pickerel, Salmon, and Perch. He brings her Grunt. He brings her Bitterling and Milkfish. He brings her Tuna.

He doesn't even ask her to gut them. He guts them himself.

She doesn't want all this fish, but fish is what he brings her. Her face is puffy from crying. She opens her whitish melancholy mouth. A little like a fish the seventh wife looks, but the husband has not realized this yet. "Did you know . . . Paul?" begins the seventh wife. She takes a few bites of Trout. "Did you know sixteenth-century natural historians classified seals, whales, amphibians, crocodiles, even hippopotamuses as fish?" She chews a little Mackerel. "Where's my hippopotamus, Paul? What were you thinking, Paul?" Paul is forever in the soup for touching and kissing and marrying those women. For all the fish he brings her there is always too much fish and there is fish missing. The seventh wife pushes some Bleak around her plate. "Where's my Seal," mutters the seventh wife grimly.

And where are ex-wives one through six now? Where are Amy and Carol and Amy, and Amy, and Carol, and Bernadette now? They are peering in through the window. They have arrived with a side dish of yams. They clutch one another and demand their fish be boiled and fried and baked and poached. They look furrier than Paul remembers. Wilder. The seventh wife pushes her Snook away. She has lost her appetite. As usual, Paul is filled with remorse. He wishes his seventh wife were a duck. The only duck swimming around in his duck pond.

THERE'S A HOLE
IN THE BUCKET

I look at the bucket. There is unquestionably a hole. An entire family could live in this hole. "I see the hole," I yell. "Call Mendelssohn." My husband, Dear Henry, calls Mendelssohn. Mendelssohn comes right over. We look at the bucket. There is a hole. Mendelssohn studies it. He takes some notes. The southernmost edge of the hole is silent, possibly frozen. The northernmost, rough and forgotten. Mendelssohn sniffs it. "Smells like gone," he says, "just as I thought." Mendelssohn cups his ear, listens to its center, and jots down: "A slight trace of harp. The bare cry of a faraway boy." "With what shall we," asks Dear Henry, "fix it?" The flower in Dear Henry's breast pocket is a pink I've never seen before. "Lean close," says Mendelssohn. We lean close. "This is going to be a nightmare." Dear Henry and I nod our heads. We know already we will need to fetch the water with a bucket to fix the hole but we will have no bucket to fetch the water to fix the hole because the bucket with which we would fetch the water has a hole. A white balloon wafts over Dear Henry's head. We are failing miserably. "With what," asks Dear Henry, "shall we fix it?" He asks again because even though we know how everything ends, the ending remains unimaginable. "With straw," says Mendelssohn, hopelessly. "With straw, I guess," says Mendelssohn again. I look around for straw. Dear Henry opens a can of sardines. He pulls back the tin lid and offers me one. "No thanks," I say. "Looking for straw," I say. He offers a sardine to Mendelssohn. "Why not," shrugs Mendelssohn. "Sardines are caught mainly at night," says Dear Henry. "I know," says Mendelssohn, chewing slowly on the fish. "They are caught when they rise to the surface to feed on plankton," says Dear Henry. "This is when they're caught," says Dear Henry. "They're caught at night when they're the hungriest." "I know," says Mendelssohn. "Everybody knows." "Except, I guess, for the sardines," says Dear Henry. Mendelssohn laughs. "It's not a joke," says Dear Henry. "Sorry," says Mendelssohn. "I'm sorry too," says Dear Henry. "For what?" asks Mendelssohn. "Just for everything," says Dear Henry. "The bucket, and the hole, and just everything." Even though I am certain when I find the straw the straw will be too long and I will need to cut the straw with an axe but the axe will be too dull and I will need to sharpen the axe with a stone but the stone will be too dry and with a hole in the bucket there is no hope for ever fetching water to wet the stone, I am nevertheless still looking around for straw. This is the song we're in. I hate this bucket. "I hate this bucket," I yell. "More than the hole?" asks Dear Henry. He looks so sad. "The hole is the hole that the hole should be. It's the bucket that's destroying us, Dear Henry. It's the bucket." I look at Mendelssohn. I mean I really look at him. Every day he looks more and more like my mother. "With what shall we fix it, Mendelssohn?" I am exhausted. How many times can a person ask the same question? Mendelssohn kneels gently beside the bucket and reaches all the way in. His dark soft curls cover his eyes. "Liza," says Dear Henry, grabbing my arm, "I think we're dying." With a stone in his hand, Mendelssohn reaches all the way into the bucket, past the hole, past god, and summer, and almonds, and shame, and the ocean, and mice, and love, and fevers, and worship, and snails, and teeth, and lilac, and forgiveness, and a song about a bucket with a hole in it, and past all the children singing the song, and past their children singing it, and their children's children, and past my broken heart until he reaches the oldest water and wets the stone. He pulls the stone out and sets it right on top of Dear Henry's head as if Dear Henry were a tombstone and I've come to his grave to mourn him. The wet stone glistens so brightly I need to cover my eyes. "With what," asks Dear Henry, "shall we . . ." I can barely hear him. The song is fading like a song. It is what it is. I remove the wet stone from the top of Dear Henry's head and bury it in my pocket. I notice that the crack shaped like a bucket on Dear Henry's cheek is spreading. There's a hole in that bucket too. I look over at Mendelssohn. He is building a whole entire city out of buckets. "There are holes in all of these," says Mendelssohn who is now covered in holes under a sky covered in holes lit by a moon covered in holes kept by prayers covered in holes.

Off in the distance, I can already see the people coming to live in Mendelssohn's City of Holes. There are so many people, and they are so beautiful and hopeful. And they too are covered in holes. They each carry a bucket. And in each bucket is a hole. This is the song we're in.

DON'T JUST DO SOMETHING, STAND THERE!

1. It all began with the milk.
2. The milk belonged to my lover, Mr. Rabinowitz.
3. For a long time something beautiful was going to happen.
4. But this was not the beautiful thing.
5. Had the milk landed on my nose as my lover, Mr. Rabinowitz, swears he had intended, we would've had a judderous laugh about it.
6. But Mr. Rabinowitz fucked up.
7. Just yesterday I accompanied my lover, Mr. Rabinowitz, to the forest.
8. How could he have forgotten so quickly?
9. I think there were thieves.

10. My lover, Mr. Rabinowitz, dipped his thumb and fore-finger into his cereal bowl and flicked the milk (that once belonged to him) at me.

11. In the forest I was frightened.

12. In the forest there were thieves.

13. In the forest my lover, Mr. Rabinowitz, showed off his wilderness skills by reciting *Waiting for Godot*.

14. "Excuse me, mister. The bones. You won't be needing the bones?"

15. But I did need the bones.

16. The milk landed not on my nose but on my newly bought, barely worn dream rush chemise.

17. My mother warned me that without the bones no one, not even Mr. Rabinowitz, my lover, who loved me one hundred times a day, would ever love me.

18. Could ever love me.

19. I needed the bones, but I could not admit to needing the bones.

20. The economy was failing and my dream rush chemise was ruined.

21. Forever?

22. Possibly forever.

23. Mr. Rabinowitz, my lover, was *just joking around*.

24. We were unemployed.

25. I heard a thud.

26. "Did you hear a thud?"

27. "It's your mother!" cheered my lover, Mr. Rabinowitz.

28. "She has come with the bones?"

29. "She has come to save us from our economic woes?"

30. "Very funny."

31. In literature a character's "fatal flaw" requires she take a metaphorical or literal plummet.

32. "Don't just do something," said my mother, "stand there!"

33. So I stood there.

34. A long time ago I wrote a book.

35. The main character's name was Beatrice.

36. Shortly after, my mother had a baby and named her Beatrice.

37. Then she had another.

38. She named that baby Beatrice too.

39. Then she had another.

40. She named that baby Beatrice too.

41. Mr. Rabinowitz, my lover, is named Mr. Rabinowitz because you cannot name a baby Mr. Rabinowitz.

42. But I did need the bones.

43. My mother took the bones away while I just stood there in my ruined chemise.

44. Would never love me.

45. Could never love me.

46. This was not the beautiful thing.

47. I was groggy with milk, which is another way of saying I was ashamed at my inability to start yelling.

48. At my mother.

49. For taking the bones.

50. At Mr. Rabinowitz.

51. For flicking the milk.

52. At all the Beatrices.

53. For not being the real Beatrice, although my mother claimed each of them to be.

54. At my mother.

55. For claiming each of them to be.

56. The real Beatrice lives in the book I wrote a long time ago.

57. The real Beatrice is terrified of nests, and string, and cashews, and Poland, and carousels for good reason.

58. There are stains that happen suddenly and can never be washed out.

59. "And if they could?"

60. "We would be saved."

61. "For god's sake," said my mother, "Mr. Rabinowitz, your lover, was *just joking around*."

62. Speaking of jokes, let me tell you a joke I once heard at a funeral.

63. His wife had died young and he told the joke at the funeral because she loved the joke, every day she loved the joke, and now he had to live a life he couldn't bear to live without her so he told the joke.

64. "What's red, hangs from a wall, and whistles?"

65. "What?"

66. "A herring."

67. "A herring? But a herring isn't red."

68. "All right! So you paint the herring red!"

69. "But a herring doesn't hang from a wall."

70. "All right! So you take a hammer and you nail the herring to the wall!"

71. "But a herring doesn't whistle."

72. "All right! So it doesn't whistle!"

73. "I don't get it."

74. "And if we dropped him? (*Pause*) If we dropped him?"

75. "He'd punish us (*Silence. He looks at the tree.*)."

76. Just yesterday I accompanied my lover, Mr. Rabinowitz, to the forest.

77. Would never love me.

78. Could never love me.

79. In the forest there were trees.

80. "I thought you said thieves," said the Beatrices.

81. The economy was failing.

82. We were unemployed.

83. "Unemployed people, Mr. Rabinowitz," said my mother, "should not be flicking milk."

84. They started kissing.

85. "Who?" asked Mr. Rabinowitz. "Who started kissing?"

86. "You and my mother."

87. "All right!" said my mother. "So we started kissing!"

88. "I don't get it," said Mr. Rabinowitz.

89. "Don't just do something," said the Beatrices, "stand there!"

90. So I stood there in my ruined chemise while my lover, Mr. Rabinowitz, and my mother kissed and kissed and kissed.

91. "You're sure you saw me, you won't come and tell me tomorrow you never saw me?"

92. "Of course not," said the real Beatrice.

93. There are stains that happen suddenly, and can never be washed out.

94. For a long time something beautiful was going to happen.

95. But this was not the beautiful thing.

96. This was the beautiful thing.

97. "I saw you," said the real Beatrice.

98. The herring started to whistle.

99. "You saw me?"

100. "I saw you."

ACKNOWLEDGEMENTS

I am thankful for support from the Sustainable Arts Foundation Award that allowed me time to complete this book.

To Danielle Dutton and Martin Riker, for this dream come true. To my oracles: Amber Dermont, Kristen Iskandrian, and Amy Margolis. Thank you for your friendship and your spells. To Will Walton, my army of one. To Avid Bookshop, one day I will write you an 800-page love letter but for now I forever salute you. To the Crying Room. To my students, thank you for the honor of bearing witness. To Wynn Walter and Kathy Setzer for guiding my sons with love and tenderness while I wrote many of these stories. And to the women of Athens who gave me a sweater when I needed it most, especially: Samara Scheckler, Hope Hilton, Shira Chess, Deirdre Sugiuchi, and Sarah Baugh.

To my father, Richard K. Mark, dear healer, thank you for always being there for me. No matter what. Rain or shine. And to my mother, Cindy Worenklein, for heaven and earth. To Jay Worenklein and Harriet Bass, the kindest, most loving stepparents in all the land.

To my grandmother, Gertrude Mark, for hearing my stories from the inside out.

To Ronnie Gorden, longtime muse.

To Ari and Etan, my brothers, my heroes. Thank you for finding me each time I go missing. To Danielle and Brielle, you inspire me over and over again.

To Eve, for your kind heart and your visions. To Sasha, my beautiful and enchanting little sister.

To Reg, without your love these stories, like me, would be wandering the flowerless field. Thank you for being my guide and my best friend. You are my home.

This book is for Noah and Eli who have rewritten my heart one thousand times bigger.

Sabrina Orah Mark is the author of *Happily* and the poetry collections *The Babies* and *Tsim Tsum*. She lives in Athens, Georgia with her husband, Reginald McKnight, and their two sons.

1. Renee Gladman *Event Factory*

2. Barbara Comyns *Who Was Changed and Who Was Dead*

3. Renee Gladman *The Ravickians*

4. Manuela Draeger *In the Time of the Blue Ball* (tr. Brian Evenson)

5. Azareen Van der Vliet Oloomi *Fra Keeler*

6. Suzanne Scanlon *Promising Young Women*

7. Renee Gladman *Ana Patova Crosses a Bridge*

8. Amina Cain *Creature*

9. Joanna Ruocco *Dan*

10. Nell Zink *The Wallcreeper*

11. Marianne Fritz *The Weight of Things* (tr. Adrian Nathan West)

12. Joanna Walsh *Vertigo*

13. Nathalie Léger *Suite for Barbara Loden* (tr. Natasha Lehrer & Cécile Menon)

14. Jen George *The Babysitter at Rest*

15. Leonora Carrington *The Complete Stories*

16. Renee Gladman *Houses of Ravicka*

17. Cristina Rivera Garza *The Taiga Syndrome* (tr. Aviva Kana & Suzanne Jill Levine)

18. Sabrina Orah Mark *Wild Milk*

19. Rosmarie Waldrop *The Hanky of Pippin's Daughter*

20. Marguerite Duras *Me & Other Writing* (tr. Olivia Baes & Emma Ramadan)

21. Nathalie Léger *Exposition* (tr. Amanda DeMarco)

22. Nathalie Léger *The White Dress* (tr. Natasha Lehrer)

23. Cristina Rivera Garza *New and Selected Stories* (tr. Sarah Booker, et al)

24. Caren Beilin *Revenge of the Scapegoat*

25. Amina Cain *A Horse at Night: On Writing*

26. Giada Scodellaro *Some of Them Will Carry Me*